EARTH'S MIGHTIEST WARRIOR

AN OLD WORLD SAGA NOVELLA

EARTH'S MIGHTIEST WARRIOR
AN OLD WORLD SAGA NOVELLA

First published April 2022.

Book cover art by warrendesign
Manuscript design by Joel Preston

ISBN 978-0-6454676-1-1 (Paperback)
ISBN 978-0-6454676-0-4 (eBook)

To contact the author email: contact@joelprestonauthor.com
joelprestonauthor.com

EARTH'S MIGHTIEST WARRIOR

AN OLD WORLD SAGA NOVELLA

JOEL PRESTON

Other Novels by This Author:

In the Shadow of Monstrous Things

Rise Golden Apollo

In the Shadow of The Old World

Fall Silver Artemis

Novellas by This Author:

The Wendigo Incident: An Old World Saga Novelette

For everyone with a warrior's spirit waiting to be freed.

ᛈᚱᛂᚤ ᛏᚧᛂ ᛁᚾᛏᚧᚨᚱ

INTRODUCTION

BY JOEL PRESTON

Before we embark on my reimagining of the epic tale of the Germanic hero Sigurd, there are some crucial points that I will cover here. There are spoilers here for those who aren't familiar with the general myth of Sigurd.

First is accuracy to the myth. While part one of the novella recreates Sigurd's tale from the Saga of the Volsungs, remember that this novella exists as a part of *The Old World Saga* - meaning specific changes have been made to the story in preparation for Sigurd's entry in the main series of books. Specifically, Sigurd's encounters with the giant Skrymir and his adventure in Utgard. These are not part of the traditional story and are my invention. To those interested in an engaging and accurate telling of Sigurd's story, I highly recommend reading or listening to '**The Saga of the Volsungs**' by **Jackson Crawford**. You cannot get a better version of the myth, and his retelling of the original stories helped immensely in shaping the first part of this novella. As a resource for wider Norse mythology, I recommend '**Norse Mythology**' by **Neil Gaiman**.

Secondly (and very importantly) is what you should read in *The Old World Saga* to best enjoy this book. While this novella is somewhat stand-alone, you will benefit greatly from having read *Rise Golden Apollo*, especially for part two of the story. Many of the characters and events mentioned come directly from *Rise Golden Apollo*. This book serves to bridge the gap (in some aspects) between that story and *The Old World Saga Book Four: Fall Silver Artemis*.

As with all mythology and religion featured in my books, I endeavour to stay as respectful to the true myth as possible; however, as in all works of fiction, sometimes the stories need to be modified to suit my own goals. In part one of this novella, you will read a semi-accurate retelling of Sigurd's early life and heroic conquests, but do not take it as a 'true-to-life' retelling of his story. The core elements are there, his conquest over the sons of Hunding, the slaying of Fafnir and his later life with Brynhild and Gudrun.

I chose to skip over the parts of Sigurd's story where Brynhild left Hindarfjoll and re-encountered Sigurd in his travels. I found these parts unnecessary to my story and somewhat confusing. I have also removed Brynhild's prophetic knowledge that Sigurd would marry Gudrun. The last primary removal is that Sigurd impersonates Gunnar for three days on top of Hindarfjoll in the original story. I couldn't see any way that Brynhild couldn't have known it was actually Sigurd, so cut it out. Again, see Crawford's book if you want the myth in full.

Regarding names in this story; for some, I have used the old Norse spelling, and for others, more modern variants. There is no rhyme or reason to this other than I liked how it looked on the page. So, if you are confused as to why Baldur is Baldr or why Grani is called Greyfell, then this is the reason.

Part two features Sigurd's adventures in the Christian Hell, which is inspired by the depiction offered in **Dante's Inferno**. However, this is my interpretation of Hell in a multi-religion world. Due to the link to Rise Golden Apollo, part one of this story takes place before the year 337AD, much earlier than the era the Volsungs are generally attributed to.

Sigurd will encounter creatures like Succubi and Japanese water demons in this story. If you haven't read *The Old World Saga* at all, I highly recommend you pick up *Rise Golden Apollo* to better understand how the Underworld looks.

I researched Norse mythology for the early chapters of part two, so I could (as accurately as possible) recreate what the Road to Hel would've looked like for people living in that time. However, my interpretation of these factual elements is modified to suit my own end. This story exists in a world where all religions co-exist, so the afterlife can never be exactly as portrayed in myth.

This novella leads straight into *Fall Silver Artemis*, with Sigurd the Volsung being a major character in that book. Treat *Earth's Mightiest Warrior* as Sigurd's origin story.

With all of that out of the way, I hope you enjoy this shorter entry into *The Old World Saga*, and look forward to Sigurd's story continuing soon!

FROM THE AUTHOR

ᚻᛁᚾ ᚲᚱᛁᛏᚻᛁᚾ

ᛋᛁᛈᛅᚱᛏᛋ ᛏᛁᛈᛁᚻᛏᛅᚱᛋ
PART ONE
ᛚᛁᛈᛁ ᚻᛏᛁ ᛏᛋᛏᛏᛪ

CHAPTER 1

SIGURD OF THE VOLSUNG LINE

King Alf paced back and forth in his well-lit hall. The blazing torchlight only served to exemplify his furrowed brow and grim expression. Troublesome thoughts gripped his mind, for his future wife was currently in labour.

Alf was younger than he looked. He had wiry silver hair and a prominent chunk missing from his nose, a reminder of a foolish skirmish in his youth. Despite his scars, he was still handsome and carried himself with a soft-spoken dignity. The woman he would marry was undoubtedly beautiful and regal. So stunning, in fact, that it seemed a miracle that she would have him. Alf whispered silent prayers to the ever-watching Aesir that by the end of this night, she would still have her life. Then she could become his in marriage.

Queen Hjordis was the most noble of women. Should she

die in childbirth, a common occurrence, Alf would know he was ill-fated by the gods.

Such was his love for Hjordis that King Alf was completely unconcerned that the child being brought into the world wasn't his. The boy, for he knew it would be a boy, was nonetheless of the highest parentage.

He was the son of Sigmund and a descendant of the legendary hero Volsung. The men of that family line were great warriors and the child would be favoured by Odin, chief of the gods, above all other mortal men.

Alf would see the boy raised well, for he would be a fearsome ally as a man. He felt the whisperings of destiny all around. This was a momentous night.

Hjordis kept the broken shards of a sword called Gram in her quarters; the blade of her former husband, Sigmund. The sword had been shattered in Sigmund's defeat.

Still, one day, those silver pieces of the legendary blade would be a mighty gift for Sigmund's son.

Alf paused and looked up at the high roof. He let memory grip him and drag him back in time.

Alf had met Hjordis leaving the site of a great battle. She'd been with a servant woman, both looking dishevelled and shaken. From their appearances, they seemed who they claimed to be.

When Alf's longships had hit the coast and his company of strong men scrambled onto the shore, it was already too late. Death was the only lingering combatant in that place.

Bodies were piled high beside broken spears and shattered shields.

Alf's company had no purpose being there other than following signs in the stars. Bright lights and new constellations high above had led Alf to that site of absolute catastrophe. In the shape of two identical ravens, the stars had shown the path to that battlefield. The fighting had been so fierce that not even the remaining armour and weapons were worth scavenging.

Desperate as he was to find meaning in his voyage, he was about to turn away when he saw the fleeing women.

Alf was a shrewd man. He'd realised all was not as it seemed when the servant spoke with the manners and grace of a highborn woman, and the highborn spoke like a commoner. A simple test deduced that Queen Hjordis, wife of Sigmund, had switched places with her servant in a poor attempt at deception.

Of course, Alf knew of the towering and war-like Sigmund. Upon discovering her identity, Alf asked Hjordis how her mighty husband had ever fallen in battle.

Hjordis stated that no man had killed Sigmund, but a god. An old man with an eye patch in a long brown cloak had walked through the soldiers, knocking them down as if they were made of clay.

Sigmund had swung at the stranger and the land was ripped asunder. The sword, Gram, shattered and Sigmund fell gravely injured.

Despair crashed across Sigmund's army like the most devastating plague, seeing them all to Valhalla shortly afterwards.

Sigmund had spoken his dying words to Hjordis moments before Alf arrived. She did not share with Alf what they had been. He figured they were something to do with the boy growing in her body.

Alf treated both women well but was so taken with Hjordis that he intended to make her his wife. As soon as the child of Sigmund was born, it would be done. She would stand alongside him as the Queen of Denmark.

•••••

Hours passed in the quiet hall. The silence was periodically broken with the howling of wolves outside.

Eventually, a servant carrying a neatly wrapped bundle approached King Alf. She passed the baby to him.

"His name is to be Sigurd," she said, bowing low.

Alf looked down at the sleeping baby. The child stirred and opened his eyes, letting out a loud wail.

Alf's mouth fell open. The boy's eyes were dazzlingly bright. In them, he saw glory and a warrior's ferocity. This child was brimming with destiny. Alf knew that this boy would have a life independent of his lands. Hjordis would be with Alf always, but this child belonged to the world.

"Sigurd," Alf smiled, "you will be the greatest of men. You will be counted first in valour, strength and accomplishments."

The baby gurgled and fell back to sleep.

•••••

As a boy, Sigurd was well loved. He grew quickly, dwarfing the other children his age. He excelled in many tasks and became a competent swordsman, rivalling the greatest warriors in Denmark before he hit his teenage years.

As was customary, Sigurd was raised by a foster father, Regin. Regin was no ordinary man; he was a dwarf from Svatralfheim. His kind were growing less and less common in Midgard (the realm of men), and Sigurd often supposed Regin could be the last of them.

Regin was short and stocky. He was old and bald on the top of his head. Where he still grew hair, around his ears and the back of his head, it fell in waterfalls of white. His beard was almost as long as his body, and the young Sigurd found great humour in watching the old man trip over it.

Despite his meek demeanour, Regin was cunning. His small grey eyes and sneering smile betrayed his constant scheming.

Yet, as a child, Sigurd didn't care for the plots of the dwarf. Regin proved to be a valuable teacher, regardless of his hidden intentions. He taught Sigurd all the usual things like sports, chess and languages. He also taught Sigurd runes – carvings with magical power.

Regin was magical and had great knowledge of the ancient symbols and the unspoken magic that permeates the world.

Regin showed Sigurd the spells that could be implanted into a rune by those with magical knowledge and ability. He taught the young warrior how to string runes together to create powerful binding spells, though Sigurd was never any good at it. Despite his divine lineage, his family line being descendants of Odin, he wasn't inherently magical.

When he was fifteen, Sigurd asked Regin if he could tattoo runes along his ribs and imbibe them with magic to aid him in future combat.

Regin agreed. The dwarf seemed to take particular joy in Sigurd's grunts and gasps as his unblemished skin was pierced with ink. His skin raw and bleeding, Sigurd didn't feel any stronger with the runic imprints running down his left rib. He wondered whether Regin had given the runes any power at all.

Despite the endless hours rolling into days and years that Sigurd and Regin spent together, a closeness never developed between them. Sigurd never knew much of Regin's history or how he came to be in the court of King Alf. He grew weary of Regin's snide comments and frequent jabs about his father's demise. The dwarf often questioned him about the riches of his ancestors, of which Sigurd knew little.

Wishing to be free of the dwarf, Sigurd volunteered to work in the royal stables. It was demanding and menial labour, though Sigurd found satisfaction in the strength he gained from it.

After spending much of his time tending to the animals, Sigurd came to wish for a horse of his own and decided to approach King Alf about it. He didn't seek Regin's advice, for he knew the dwarf to be scared of horses.

• • • • •

On a summer's day, when the sun hung high and the wildflowers were in full bloom, Sigurd went to the king. Alf leaned back in his chair. His hair was thinning, yet he maintained a regal image. He fixed his eyes to Sigurd as the young man approached.

Sigurd appeared to be a man, though he was still just a boy.

He had a muscular physique with a barrel chest and legs like tree trunks. The muscles on his arms were large enough to choke a wild boar. He was seven feet tall, standing above all other men. His long blonde hair was wild and his eyes a piercing blue.

"My Lord," Sigurd started, kneeling before Alf's throne, "I wish to request a horse of my own."

Alf beckoned Sigurd to rise and laughed. "Sigurd, my boy, you do not have to request such things. If you wish for a horse, any horse, from my stables, just take it!"

Sigurd was pleased with this response. Despite his time in the stables moving hay and shovelling manure, he hadn't considered which horse he'd like to call his own.

"And if I wish for a horse from the wild?" Sigurd asked tentatively.

"Sigurd, you are only fifteen, and yet you stand mightier than any beast you could come across. I suspect gangs of brigands would run from you. Scour the countryside for all I care, but I suspect you will find no horses greater than mine."

Sigurd bowed low. Without another word, he set off in the direction of the stables.

"A man should have a fine horse," he thought. *"I will find a beast that will serve me in war and adventure equally."*

‹HAPTER 2

ᏀREYFELL

It was afternoon when Sigurd walked through the stables. The old shelter of rotten wood, perpetually overwhelmed with droppings, was bathed in a lazy orange glow. There were many proud and noble stallions, yet they all seemed to be missing a quality Sigurd desired. A quality he couldn't quite define. He found more interest in determining the rotten wooden panels he'd soon need to replace.

Feeling defeated, Sigurd sat on a bale of hay, unable to choose a horse.

His mind drifted to the wild country.

The stables sat on the outer perimeter of the castle beside a forest of untamed tangled trees. When a branch snapped on the forest's edge, Sigurd jumped to his feet. He grabbed a long wooden stick from the ground and scanned the tree line for bandits or marauders.

A hooded figure moved in the shadows.

"Reveal yourself!" Sigurd boomed in his powerful voice.

The shadow moved again, setting off at a bristling pace into the forest.

Sigurd snarled and bolted after him, leaping across rocks and darting around trees with speed and agility not suited to his muscular frame.

Sunlight split the trees ahead and Sigurd jumped into a clearing, sending leaves fluttering.

The figure before him wore a simple hooded brown robe. He was tall, though not as tall as Sigurd.

"Turn around and let me gaze upon you," Sigurd commanded.

"A boy of fifteen without a hair on his chin would command me," an unfamiliar voice chuckled. Sigurd was immediately taken aback. The words had been kind yet radiated authority.

The robed man turned and lowered his hood. It was just an old man with an eye patch and a long silvery beard. Curiously, a jet-black raven flew from a high tree branch to land on his shoulder.

The old man petted it absent-mindedly and observed Sigurd with his one good eye.

"I'm Sigurd," Sigurd said, failing to sound imposing.

"I know who you are and what you seek. Come with me, boy. We will find a field that sits beside the River Busiltjorn. There are horses yet unbroken by men there."

With a swift turn, the old man marched into the clump of trees before them. Sigurd followed, still gripping the stick he'd picked upright.

When they emerged in the field, Sigurd was amazed to see

a herd of majestic horses prancing through the long grass. Any would have been a fine beast to tame, but one stood out more than the others. Near the centre of the herd was a grey stallion with dark eyes and a long black tail. He looked powerful and fast.

"Drive the herd into the river, where the water is fast and dangerous. See the noblest horse reveal itself," the old man said, sitting on a nearby stone.

Sigurd took a deep breath and ran towards the herd, bellowing as he did so. The horses reared up in alarm and made for the edge of the field, where Sigurd could hear water rushing.

Sigurd clapped his hands and roared.

The horses stepped nervously into the water, their fear of Sigurd outweighing their fear of the river.

The herd crossed, battling against the current.

When Sigurd reached the stony shore, he found all the horses on the further river bank, bar one.

The young grey stallion stood in the deepest part of the river, defiantly facing him. It was as if the horse didn't care about the dangers of the current at all.

The old stranger appeared at Sigurd's side and handed him a length of rope. The young man tied a simple knot and created a lasso. The old man stopped him when he moved to throw it around the horse's neck.

"Would this horse be your servant or your equal?" the stranger smiled. The raven on his shoulder squawked loudly.

"What would you have me do?" Sigurd asked.

"Swim into the river and meet him. Offer him the rope, and if he finds you worthy, he will come back to shore."

Sigurd eyed the swirling rapids with apprehension. He looked into the stallion's dark eyes and saw his defiant fire staring at the pair on the bank.

Without another thought, Sigurd stepped into the water.

It pulled at him, threatening to wash him away. He lost his footing and went under, emerging with a splutter. He swam against the current, his powerful arms overcoming the river's force.

Near the middle, it shallowed. Drenched and out of breath, Sigurd's feet found a tall rock and he stood beside the stallion.

He held the rope before him.

"We will be equals, you and I. Together we will ride to war and make history."

The horse's long eyelashes fluttered as it blinked, then it lowered its head.

Not yet confident of mounting the horse, Sigurd threw the rope around its neck and began swimming towards shore.

Soon, both man and stallion were standing by the edge of the field.

"A powerful steed," the old man said curiously. "What will you name him?"

"I will name him Greyfell," Sigurd said, stroking the horse's neck.

"This horse matches its rider," the old man laughed.

"How so?" Sigurd asked.

"He is a descendant of Sleipnir, the horse of Odin. There will be no greater horse for you to mount."

Sigurd knew of Sleipnir, the eight-legged stallion that Odin rode. He was said to be faster and stronger than all horses.

Sigurd turned back to Greyfell and studied him intently. There was no doubt that this was a remarkable beast, both sleek and strong. His mane shone with the blackness of the night.

"Keep this horse well nourished and see him never falter," the old man stated.

"How do you know Greyfell's ancestry?" Sigurd asked.

No one responded. The old man was gone, having vanished into thin air.

It was then that Sigurd knew he had been speaking with Odin.

"Come, Greyfell. The stables are not worthy of your magnificence. I will build you your own stable near the woods. Then I will learn to be a master horseman. When war comes, as it surely will, you and I will find victory together."

Greyfell whinnied, and they set off back towards the forest and the distant castle of Alf.

CHAPTER 3

REGIN'S REQUEST

Sigurd did as he'd said. He had no skill in the art of carpentry. Still, fortunately, his popularity among the common folk meant many came forward to assist him.

Sigurd learned to fell trees and shape the wood. Metalworkers and smiths created joins and fixings for him, and in time they made a kingly stable for Greyfell.

Sigurd was surprised as he found a simple joy in the building of the structure. His large calloused hands worked tirelessly as his sense of satisfaction grew.

Regin often watched Sigurd from afar over those long summer months, a look of curiosity mingled with disgust on his face.

Sigurd already knew Regin's thoughts on the matter. A highborn man shouldn't spend so much time with common folk, but Sigurd didn't care.

He took to riding Greyfell as much as he could. The horse carried loads far greater than an average horse, and his speed didn't dim in heavy snow.

In the years that followed, whenever King Alf entertained foreigners in his court, Sigurd took the opportunity to learn from them. He mastered horse combat with sword and spear.

By Sigurd's eighteenth birthday, he was bulky, bearded and fearsome. He was ready to fight.

Though, much to his disappointment, Alf had no enemies. So instead, during long walks through the shadows of the woods, he thought about his father.

Alf explained that Sigmund's army had been defeated by enemies from a far distant land. They were the sons of Hunding, five kings led by a man named Lyngvi. Lyngvi had wealth beyond measure that Sigurd felt was his for the taking.

One day, as he sat in the stables beside Greyfell thinking about Sigmund's stolen treasure, Regin approached.

Sigurd's tunic was coated in muck and grime from the day's riding. An unexpected fall had left twigs tangled in his long blonde hair.

"Look at you, boy," Regin growled, shaking his head. "If I did not know your birth, I would think you a lowly peasant."

"A peasant of my size and strength you have never seen," Sigurd laughed, clapping Regin on the back.

"It is unbecoming of you to live the way you are. You are a man in all but experience."

Sigurd frowned. Regin was right.

"What would you have me do?" Sigurd asked.

Regin smiled wickedly.

"I know of a horde of treasure that, were you to claim it, would bring you wealth and recognition beyond imagining. The most famous of kings could not brag about having more gold than you."

Sigurd looked down at Regin, studying the dwarf intently. He could not say that he wasn't intrigued.

"Speak plainly and let your words fall on willing ears," Sigurd said, sitting on a wooden barrel.

"What do you know of dragons?" Regin asked, his eyes positively gleaming.

"I know of them in basic size and shape, but very little else. Does a dragon guard this treasure horde?"

"Yes," Regin said. "He is known as Fafnir and he lives in a place called Gnitaheath."

"I have heard of Fafnir. Rumour states that he is so monstrous in size that none dare go near him. How big is this creature?"

"Oh, average size," Regin shrugged. Sigurd suspected that he was trying to downplay it a little.

"I have no claim to this dragon's treasure horde," Sigurd said, sensing treachery from Regin.

"Your ancestors look upon you with shame. Those of the Volsung bloodline are the most noble and courageous of men, yet here you shrink away from promised glory," Regin said.

Sigurd was incensed. It was as if Regin's insult had lit a fire under him. Yet, he could not escape his suspicion that the dwarf had his own goals in discussing this treasure.

"Calm down," Regin continued dismissively. "I will tell you my tale, and you will see that this cause is just."

Sigurd unclenched his fists and sat back atop the uncomfortable barrel.

"Where do I begin?" muttered Regin, scratching his chin. He strode back and forth, murmuring to himself, lost in memory.

"My father was named Hreidmar. He lived on an estate in Midgard yet wore many powerful objects forged in Svartlfheim. He had three sons, Fafnir, the largest and most brutal of us; Otter, the shape-shifter; and myself.

"I am ashamed to say I was the most meagre of Hreidmar's children. Yet my skill in working iron, silver and gold was such that I could always create something new. Otter often spent his day in the form of an otter as he swam the rivers hunting for food. This would be his undoing, for as an otter does, he would eat with his eyes closed.

"There came a day that the Aesir were walking along the bank near where Otter was eating. They were Odin, chief of all gods, Loki and Hoenir. Seeing Otter's eyes closed, completely unaware, the trickster Loki threw a stone and killed him. The gods considered this to be a lucky thing. Loki then skinned Otter and made his pelt into a bag.

"That night, the three gods came to Hreidmar's estate. When we saw the bag slung over Loki's shoulder, we knew at once it was our kinsman. My father bellowed with rage as Fafnir, with his brute strength, bound the gods in dwarven chains. Hreidmar demanded to know who had killed Otter.

"Loki   admitted   to   this   deed,   understanding   that compensation needed to be paid. Hreidmar asked for gold enough to fill the Otter skin bag inside and completely cover the outside."

Sigurd snorted derisively. An otter wasn't a large animal.

"You forget, boy," Regin started, his eyes deadly, "that Otter was a shape-shifter. The bag from his skin was magical, able to fit enormous amounts inside.

"At once, Loki knew there was only one treasure horde on Midgard large enough to satiate Hreidmar's demands. The treasure of Andvari."

Regin was clearly waiting for Sigurd to gasp in response at this revelation. Sigurd had never heard of Andvari, so he remained motionless, listening.

"Andvari was cursed to live as a fish. His story is one I will not go into now. But it is needed to know that he kept his treasure behind a large waterfall. Loki borrowed a net and went from waterfall to waterfall looking for Andvari. As it turns out, Loki found Andvari where he had initially killed Otter. In his net, Loki caught Andvari and demanded the gold.

"In exchange for his life, Andvari directed Loki to the treasure horde, and Loki took every piece of it. There were many powerful rings in that horde. Loki was captivated by one golden ring in particular, called Andvaranaut. So much so that he pocketed it, intending to keep it."

"What is so special about Andvaranaut?" Sigurd asked.

"It is not special to look upon. It is a simple ring lined with faint runes. While easy to dismiss on the outside, the ring holds power above all others. From nothing, it can create gold, and where there is treasure, the ring can multiply it. Should the poorest man find that ring, he could be rich beyond all others within a day.

"When Loki returned to my father's estate, he deposited the treasure in and around the bag until there was nothing but a mound of glittering gems and gold. Fafnir and I were happy, yet my father saw one whisker still protruding from the pile. Reluctantly, Loki took Andvaranaut from his pocket and covered the whisker.

"Sourly, he looked upon us and said that the Aesir had paid a high price that day and that the treasure would only lead to misery and death. A curse from Loki is nothing to be trifled with. I suspect of all the treasures in that horde, Andvaranaut is the most cursed. But that is just my speculation. Loki's utterings may have just been disgruntled words from an annoyed god.

"After this, we let the gods depart. Though Fafnir and I were due compensation as much as my father, Hreidmar decided all the treasure would be his.

"Fafnir was taken with the golden pile. So much that he went to sleep that night gazing at it while he lay on the floor. When my father woke, Fafnir cut off his head and claimed every coin, ring and jewel as his own."

Regin looked particularly sour.

"Fafnir was a dwarf like you then? How did he become a dragon?" Sigurd asked.

"The gold corrupted him. As Fafnir fixated on it, he grew in size, so much so that he had to move the treasure from the house. His words became poison as he stretched and contorted into a serpent. He moved his treasure into a cave where he would sleep upon it every night. I followed him to this cave in secret."

"I am sorry for what you have been through," Sigurd said

solemnly. "Your kinsmen are evil to deny you compensation so deserved."

Regin nodded in a matter-of-fact way.

"After this, I left and wandered the world, coming to King Alf's court. Then fate brought you to me, a man who at last had the potential to slay the evil Fafnir."

"Use your skill as a smith to craft me a sword greater than any before. If my courage serves me, I will perform great deeds with it and slay this dragon."

"I trust you will keep your word in this matter," Regin said. "I will go to the forge and begin now."

Sigurd followed the dwarf to the forge; his excitement made him focus on nothing else.

Sigurd watched as Regin worked the forge with the legendary skill of dwarves. Long had they been renowned as masters of metalwork and Regin was no exception. Steam billowed up as the dwarf completed a gleaming broadsword and passed it to Sigurd.

Without a moment's hesitation, Sigurd swung the sword straight into the side of the huge iron anvil. The blade shattered on impact.

"You will try again," Sigurd frowned, and Regin looked disgruntled.

"Let me work in peace," Regin said, turning back to the forge.

Sigurd departed, attending to his stable duties for the day.

Reeking of horse manure, he returned in the late afternoon to test the dwarf's second attempt.

Again, the blade splintered into fragments when it hit the

anvil.

"I will accept no such blade," Sigurd said, surveying the shining pieces on the ground.

Regin looked both incredibly annoyed and insulted. He stroked at his long grey beard, then his eyes lit up as an idea came to him.

"Tell me, boy, does your mother still have the pieces of your father's sword."

Sigurd nodded.

"Fetch them, and I will forge a sword that will cleave this anvil in two."

Sigurd did as requested, finding his mother Hjordis alone in a small chamber.

"Mother, I wish to ask something of you," Sigurd began.

Hjordis smiled and beckoned her son to sit.

"I require the fragments of my father's sword to create a weapon of my own."

"I knew this day would come. Go to my bed-chamber, and you will find them wrapped in cloth in the wooden chest of drawers. Be careful, time has not dulled the sharpness of the blade."

Sigurd found the bundle and delivered it to Regin, who promptly set about creating his third and final blade.

The sound of hammer on iron rang through the forge as the dwarf became a mighty silhouette in the orange glow.

When at last the weapon was ready, Regin called for Sigurd.

"This is Gram," Regin said, pointing at the ornate blade on a nearby bench. It shone with an unworldly light and its brown hilt was inscribed with Nordic runes.

Sigurd gently wrapped his fingers around the hilt's leather bindings. It felt like this sword had always belonged in his hand. There was something of home about it.

Without a second thought, Sigurd again swung at the anvil.

In a shower of sparks, the blade cut cleanly into the solid object, cutting it right down the middle.

Sigurd grinned.

"You will kill Fafnir now?" Regin asked excitedly.

Sigurd felt a sudden swell of purpose holding Gram.

"First, I will avenge my father. I cannot fight a dragon before I have fought in a war. When I return, be rest assured; I will slay the dragon Fafnir."

Regin opened his mouth to argue, but Sigurd stopped him.

"It does not sit right with me, now that I have my horse and sword, that your father should be avenged before mine."

Regin had no choice but to agree. He did look somewhat sour as Sigurd swung Gram back and forth.

"A remarkable blade this is, Regin. You honour me, and you honour yourself with this fine piece of work," Sigurd said, struggling to keep the joy and awe out of his voice.

"Go now to King Alf. Ask him for an army to see your desire for vengeance satiated. Then we can get onto the business of Fafnir," Regin stated.

Sigurd nodded formally at his teacher, then turned and strode out of the forge, Gram swinging at his side.

Sigurd was ready at last for war.

CHAPTER 4

WAR

There was another of Sigurd's family who dwelled in the court of King Alf, though he was rarely seen in public. Gripir, Sigurd's maternal uncle, was a figure shrouded in mystery. He was gifted with the ability to see along the lifeline of men and tell their futures.

Unsure how he should begin his quest to avenge his father, Sigurd sought a meeting with Gripir.

Sigurd's uncle dwelled in a simple wooden hut in a dense part of the forest near the castle. Strange exotic smells drifted from the ever-burning fires inside. Assorted herbs and plants hung in clumps around the exterior, bathed in the smoke that wafted out through slits in the walls.

With Gram safely sheathed in its scabbard, Sigurd approached the rustic cabin and pushed the door open, breathing the perfumed air in deep.

Gripir looked at Sigurd as if his entry hadn't been a surprise.

The mystic gazed at Sigurd with his sunken black eyes.

In the centre of his hut was a substantial metal pit alive with burning coals and reaching flames. It was hard to see through the haze of smoke that clung to the inside walls.

"On the eve of battle, mighty Sigurd approaches his uncle to see what the future might hold," Gripir croaked, throwing a handful of white rocks into the fire.

"Uncle, my mind is readied. The time to avenge the deaths of Sigmund and his army has come," Sigurd said.

"Yes, yes," Gripir muttered. The orange glow from the fire pit cast ominous shadows across his face.

"What wisdom do you have to give?" Sigurd asked, sitting for some relief from the smoke.

"I have looked into your life and have seen something I have never seen before. Heroism, war, glory, and all that is expected awaits you on your chosen path. But there is also treachery and death."

"That does not sound any different from the lives of many men," Sigurd shrugged.

"No, though your star shines higher in the sky than that of any other. I have seen that after death comes life anew, though I cannot explain it. Time will pass as the world changes beyond imagining, and Sigurd will walk into battle again."

"What does this vision mean?"

"That, I cannot tell. What I see of your distant fate is blurred and unclear. This is something I have only ever encountered before when lives get heavily involved with the divine."

Sigurd felt that Gripir might be losing his touch.

"Let us forget far off futures and return to the present. As to my quest to wage war on foreign lands, what should I do?"

"Go to King Alf and seek his aid. See all that is asked, granted. Leave this place a boy and return a man."

The fire glowed with a sudden burst of intensity, then dimmed.

Sigurd nodded formally, then departed Gripir's hut. He headed straight for Alf's castle.

Gaining an audience with the king at once, Sigurd bowed low and made his request.

"I hold you in the highest honour. You have loved me as your son, yet you and I know you are not my father. I think it is time that the sons of Hunding, who defeated my father Sigmund those long years ago, now learn that not all the Volsungs are dead."

Without so much as a pause, Alf ordered riders to go to his bannermen with one message: war is coming.

"Within two weeks, we will have an army ready to sail," he grinned.

Sigurd felt his heart beat a little faster in the excitement.

"Will you come and fight with me in foreign lands?" Sigurd asked.

"No," Alf replied. "This is your war and your glory shouldn't be shared. Command your men, fight well, and return with news of victory. In return, I ask you to bring the spoils of war to my castle in payment for the soldiers I have given you."

Sigurd, having always expected this to be the case, agreed readily.

A fleet of dragon boats was assembled, with Sigurd being

gifted the largest and finest of them all.

Regin was overwhelmed with work as men from the countryside requested armour and weapons, all wishing to aid Sigurd in his cause.

Though not as great a gift as the mighty sword Gram, Regin forged a helmet and shield for Sigurd of unmatched quality. The helmet was full-faced with an iron beard and large wings jutting from either side of its dome. The shield was wooden but lined with iron and carried an image of the helmet on its front face.

Sigurd's blazing bright eyes shone through the helmet, creating an awe-inspiring visage.

Sigurd met his generals, each an experienced warrior who would guide him through the coming conflict.

When the moon was due to rise high and full in the sky, Sigurd's army set sail.

Once they hit open water, they were assaulted with a rough sea. Waves smashed into boats and fearsome winds threatened to blow their sails away.

"Raise the sails higher!" Sigurd commanded. "Our first foe is this storm, and, in its face, we will show our courage!"

The ominous weather didn't abate for several days.

They came past a rocky precipice where a solitary figure stood, watching the fleet sail past.

"Who has rallied such an army?" the lone man yelled.

"Sigurd, Sigmund's son!" the men on the nearest dragon boat called back.

"Pass word to your commander that if he would have me aboard, the foul weather will leave you."

Word carried quickly to Sigurd, who ordered his ship close to the rocks so that the stranger could join them.

Once aboard, Sigurd eyed the man warily and asked, "Who are you?"

"Call me Spellcaster," the man said. His face was wrapped in bandages, leaving only one eye visible. He wore a long black travelling cloak, with chainmail sleeves visible beneath.

"Why have you asked to come aboard my ship?"

"I was there when great Volsung set a table for the ravens. It is a good omen to have me aboard. I have heard that Sigurd is the foremost of all young men."

And so Spellcaster joined Sigurd as they journeyed on. As the stranger had promised, they were met only with clear skies and helpful winds from that moment on.

They discussed military strategy for many days. With each conversation, Sigurd grew more excited for war.

When they came to land at last, Sigurd was first onto the beach.

Fire and death to the realm of the sons of Hunding. Sigurd's army laid waste to towns and decimated the small bands of defenders that came against them.

Early victories bolstered his army of filthy fighting men. Chainmail was cut, shields were bashed and axes were hewn in half. The aggression of Sigurd's army was matched by the people of these lands, though they didn't have the same skill to save themselves.

Many of the battle-hardened veterans in Alf's army said they had never seen a man fight with the ferocity of Sigurd. Men fled when they fell into Sigurd's tall shadow. Gram took the lives of many soldiers as it cleaved the land now soaked in blood.

Survivors fled to the court of King Lyngvi and warned him that a mighty host, led by the son of Sigmund, was here to conquer and burn. They described Sigurd as a bright-eyed giant who wore a cloak of his enemies' blood.

Lyngvi summoned a mighty army of his own. He was a noble man who would not flee his own lands. He may have been old, but he was no coward. His war summons carried far and wide.

Soon an army greater than Sigurd's in number was gathered.

Still, as the months of minor conflicts raged on, the sons of Hunding came to regret ancient boasts that the line of Volsung had been finished at their hands. Sigurd's war machine was an unstoppable juggernaut, rolling across rivers and mountains, squashing the realm beneath it.

Sigurd was said to inspire such loyalty that his men would rise and keep fighting beside him even when pierced with a dozen arrows. The legends being born sent a wave of fear through Lyngvi's ranks.

• • • • •

Word reached Sigurd of Lyngvi's formidable army when Sigurd's forces halted for the night at the edge of a wide valley near a small village.

A scout stated plainly that the two forces would meet within a week if they were to continue marching westward.

Word moved quickly through the camp, and a wave of restlessness fell over the men.

Seeking distraction, Sigurd went into the village. He and his generals were pleasantly surprised to find a welcoming homestead where a barman offered generous mugs of home-brewed mead.

The barman stated plainly that Sigurd's army would be most welcome to drink and feast here if they left the valley in peace.

Sigurd saw the eagerness in his men's eyes and agreed.

Caught in the swell of victory and the success of their campaign so far, Sigurd even encouraged his men to enter the longhouse and drink to their heart's content.

The place was soon filled with boisterous laughter and the clunking of mugs against each other as the warriors cheered to the coming death of Lyngvi and the sons of Hunding.

Spellcaster raised his mug to Sigurd and said, "Already your legend has been born. But even now, Lyngvi summons an army greater in strength than yours. These men are experienced and hardy. The fight that determines victory in this campaign will not be yours so easily."

Sigurd grunted in response. He sipped at his mug and watched the barman curiously.

His eyes flicked to his generals and the other men who now filled the longhouse.

"We fight for honour, Spellcaster," Sigurd began, "but there is equal honour, I think, in this. The brewing of mead and the bringing of joy. Fighting men need such things, don't you think?"

"You are not wrong, Sigurd. Yet you are not destined to live such a life. Your glory will come through courage and war. Sigurd as a barman is an amusing thought, though."

"It is a shame that we must walk the path set before our

feet. In another life, perhaps I would brew fine drinks and bring joy not through bloodshed but through a place like this."

Spellcaster gave Sigurd an odd look. Then, he laughed.

"You truly are different, Sigurd. Men of war are often only occupied by thoughts of war. To see beyond such things makes you whole. But, do not let such thoughts distract you, this life is not for you."

Sigurd's mind wandered back to the building of Greyfell's stables. He could build a place similar in design to this one.

"Maybe in another life," Sigurd thought, then took a hearty swig from his drink.

• • • • •

A few days later, the final battle of the campaign took place. The forces of King Lyngvi and the sons of Hunding, the very same who had so long ago defeated Sigmund, faced Sigurd's army from across a wide-open field. The air was so thick with tension and expectancy it could be cut with a sword.

Men on horseback waving tall banners moved to the front of the procession. Sigurd's forces were dirty and tired from months of marching and fighting. Lyngvi's men were clean and refreshed, their eyes burning with the determination of those desperate to defend their homeland.

Sigurd, on Greyfell, moved to the front of his line. He brandished Gram, the sword's silver blade gleaming in the morning light.

"My brothers, my friends," Sigurd bellowed. "We have

fought and bled together. We have brought glory to every man's family. Long ago, King Lyngvi came to my father's lands. The sons of Hunding slaughtered their way to victory. This day, with my father's re-forged sword in hand, we will repay that debt owed in blood!"

An enormous roar came up from Sigurd's army.

"The riches stolen from me will be reclaimed so that you all may live in a prosperous kingdom for the rest of your days!"

Horns blew. Sigurd pointed his sword across the field and muttered, "For Sigmund."

He charged, with his cavalry close behind.

From Lyngvi's ranks came a hail of arrows, so black and dense that they blotted the sky.

Horses bellowed and men cried out in agony as they fell dead.

Greyfell, with speed and precision, avoided the deadly falling points and ploughed first into Lyngvi's ranks, with a lack of fear only the noblest of horses could show.

When Greyfell's advance was slowed, Sigurd leapt from his horse onto a crowd of soldiers, quickly cutting their throats and getting to his feet. His sword flew furiously back and forth.

Sigurd's men clashed with Lyngvi's front line, and the ground was soaked red. The fighting was fierce and evenly matched.

Once the ground troops had pushed past Sigurd's position, he mounted Greyfell again and hastened to aid the cavalry, who were being shot down by archers.

Heads left bodies as Sigurd and Greyfell subdued the lines of archers, leaving his horsemen to rally and launch a counterattack.

Sigurd felt the stinging bite of two arrows, one in his upper chest and the other in his left arm. Neither was a fatal blow.

Spellcaster found him and wrapped cloth around the wounds.

"Sigurd, they are a foe equal to us, yet they have numbers! You must find the king and dishearten them with his death!"

Sigurd nodded. He handed Spellcaster Greyfell's reigns and said, "I will walk to Lyngvi and cut down every man who stands between us."

The stings from the arrows filled Sigurd with an unquenchable thirst for violence and victory. He stood taller and larger than all other men, and waded into the thick of the fighting like an army unto himself.

Men fled in terror before him as he defeated every foe that crossed his path. Blood soaked armour and limbs removed from bodies showed Sigurd's path through the fight.

When the midday sun sat high above the corpse-laden field, Sigurd faced Lyngvi.

There was no talk.

Their eyes met and Sigurd beckoned the king to face him.

First came Lyngvi's brother, running at Sigurd with madness in his eyes.

Sigurd, soaked in blood and holding Gram tight, struck a mighty blow and cut the man cleanly in two.

Lyngvi spat at the ground, though he still did not say a word.

The two men approached each other, the other surviving

sons of Hunding watching nervously.

Their blades clashed with a fearsome screech of metal.

Sigurd broke the parry and turned, ducking slightly, as he spun around.

Lyngvi jumped backwards to avoid the blow but lost his balance as his feet landed against his brother's torso.

Sigurd swung again, bringing his sword down on Lyngvi's helmet. Armour, chainmail, flesh and bone splintered as Gram cut down into the king's body, and he fell dead.

The other sons of Hunding died shortly after, failing to inflict any injury on Sigurd.

Lyngvi's army faltered, and his men died in numbers beyond counting.

When at last the scene was still, save for the flapping of crows above, Sigurd roared in victory. His father was avenged.

• • • • •

The coming weeks saw Sigurd's army claim the realm's treasures and prepare them for transport back to Denmark.

He ensured that his forces inflicted no more damage on the people of that land, claiming it under his rule. Spellcaster requested that he be left to manage the region in Sigurd's stead until Sigurd was ready to be a king. Sigurd agreed, trusting Spellcaster.

Then, his heart packed with triumph, he departed and returned to King Alf's court.

After many days of feasting were done, Sigurd, at last, found himself alone in the stables by the forest tending to Greyfell.

Shuffling footsteps approached, and without looking up, Sigurd knew who had come.

"Regin," Sigurd said.

"The boy returns a man."

Regin spoke with the eagerness of a person who'd been waiting a long time for this moment.

"You have avenged your father. You must now keep the vow you swore and help me avenge mine."

"I will do as promised," Sigurd said. "I will rest this night, then in the morning will make for the dragon's lair."

Regin rubbed his hands together and grinned, his small eyes glinting wickedly.

⟨HAPTER 5

DRAGON SLAYER

As the rising sun ignited the world in a blaze of orange and purples, Sigurd mounted Greyfell.

Regin had managed to find a speckled-grey pony to ride, finding Sigurd's suggestion that he could share Greyfell's saddle insulting. The dwarf had forged horseshoes that he assured Sigurd would allow the pony to keep up with the stallion. Sigurd privately thought that no horse, magically-shoed or otherwise, could match his.

Gnitaheath was a seven day journey south. Regin stated that it wasn't far from the Rhine River, and at the river they'd find Fafnir's tracks.

Sigurd had packed for a more extended expedition. He had a feeling in his gut that this would be the last time he'd look upon King Alf's court. Sigurd was scarred and battle-hardened, ready to take on the world.

They moved through the wilds, stopping at the small villages they found along the way. The odd pair drew a lot of attention from the common folk, who ogled at the gigantic blonde man in his winged helmet beside the elderly dwarf.

They encountered no trouble, not from brigand or bear on those lonely roads.

On the morning of the eighth day, they came to a place by the river where the grass was mangled and the trees bent at odd angles as if a considerable force had knocked them askew.

Sigurd frowned.

"Regin," he started slowly, "long ago, you told me that Fafnir was not so large. But judging by the path his belly has scraped in the earth, he is of considerable size."

"In his endless greed, the dragon must've grown," Regin shrugged, observing the large clawed footprints in the ground.

"And how would I slay a beast of such magnitude?" Sigurd asked.

"You will dig a hole, of course. Submerge yourself in it and stab my brother in the heart as he slithers above you."

"What will happen if the dragon's blood spills on me?"

Regin raised his hands in the air and said in a mocking, crying voice, "Oh, there's just no getting you to do anything, is there? Are you sure you are a descendant of Volsung? In your conquest against the sons of Hunding, did you run and hide behind large rocks instead of fighting?"

Sigurd drew Gram threateningly. Anger blazed in his eyes.

With a yelp, Regin ran away as fast as his little legs could carry him.

Glad to be temporarily free from the dwarf, Sigurd moved away from the river. He soon came to an abandoned stone village. The buildings were all in a state of disrepair. As Fafnir's path moved right through the centre of the place, Sigurd was sure it was the dragon that had turned a couple of the simple houses into piles of rubble.

Still, Regin's plan had been good. A hole in the earth could easily be disguised among the loosely-strewn stone. Fafnir's path climbed up a small cliff, meaning this was as far as Sigurd was going to go anyway.

He began to dig. The mid-morning sun hung high in the crystal blue sky when he'd finished a trench large enough for him to fit in. He climbed down into it and thrust his sword upwards, pretending the belly of the beast was there now.

"I don't think this will do," a familiar voice said.

Sigurd clambered out of the hole and looked in amazement at who he saw. It was not Regin but the old man he'd met once in the forest by King Alf's castle.

It was the chief of the Aesir, Odin.

"I see Greyfell is well-nourished and strong," the one-eyed god smiled. He wore a long travelling cloak and a wide-brimmed hat.

"Lord Odin," Sigurd said, bowing his head slightly.

"This trench will be the death of you," Odin said, stroking his beard.

Sigurd saw that his fingers were lined with golden rings of unworldly beauty.

"I would stab at the dragon from below as he passes,"

Sigurd stated, unsure of himself.

"And, if you do so, you will drown in blood. An unpleasant death."

"What must I do?" Sigurd asked.

"Dig several more pits with a canal to each. Let the blood drain away from you."

Sigurd grimaced.

"We will not meet again Sigurd, Sigmund's son," Odin said, rather cheerily.

"Perhaps in Valhalla," Sigurd stated.

"Die a heroic death in battle with your sword in your hand and it may be so," Odin said. Then, with a swish of his cloak, he vanished.

Sigurd continued labouring for several more hours as he dug further pits and channels. He had only just finished when he felt the earth begin to move.

Booming tremors shook the land and Sigurd scrambled into the first hole.

A tremendous roar rang across the countryside as Fafnir descended the cliff and marched towards the river, poison spewing in a purple cloud before him.

Sigurd popped his head up to take in the horrific appearance of the dragon.

Fafnir was dark grey, with a squashed head and small reptilian eyes. He looked like a great wingless slug with four powerful legs. His long neck and tail thrashed about, uprooting trees and sending boulders flying.

Sigurd could barely comprehend the size of the creature.

He was enormous, so enormous he had to be the largest thing in the world.

Sigurd waited patiently for the dragon to slither above; Gram held at the ready.

When the sun was blocked and Sigurd was cast in deep shadow, he knew it was time.

With a mighty thrust, Sigurd forced his sword upwards. There was a squelch, and blood rained into the pit in a crimson waterfall.

Fafnir screeched and reared up. Sigurd, whose hand didn't dare release his grip on the hilt of Gram, was flung from the hole and into the open air.

He landed hard on his back.

Rallying instantly, Sigurd got to his feet and took in one deep breath of air as a cloud of poison washed over him. He knew he had about two minutes to finish this fight before his lungs faltered. Already the poison burned his eyes and blistered his skin.

Fafnir's large jaws of misshapen teeth snapped at him, and Sigurd rolled out of the way. He placed one hand against Fafnir's scaly hide and the other on the hilt of Gram, still embedded in the dragon's flesh.

He pulled the sword free, creating a spurting fountain of blood.

Fafnir rolled, his lumbering body threatening to squash Sigurd.

Fortunately, he was able to jump into one of his drainage pits right as the colossal body slammed down above him.

Once Fafnir had passed, he pulled himself out. He needed

to breathe.

Sigurd heard a whinny, and Greyfell came galloping from the nearby trees. Sigurd held out an arm and caught his horse by the reigns, pulling himself onto the saddle.

Briefly free of the poisonous cloud, Sigurd took a much-needed breath and steeled his nerve.

He directed Greyfell back to Fafnir. Greyfell rose to his hind legs, kicking his front hooves at Fafnir's head. The dragon shot his elastic neck forward, threatening to swallow horse and rider whole.

Greyfell darted to the side and galloped at an astonishing pace. Sigurd raised Gram and ran the blade along Fafnir's back. His hide was so thick and magical that the sword couldn't pierce it.

Sigurd leapt from Greyfell and commanded the horse away. Fafnir's eyes followed the horse, seeing an easy meal. The dragon was well within striking distance of the grey stallion.

Sigurd dove into another of his pits as the dragon reared up, then slammed down, extending his neck towards Greyfell.

Dust and stones rocketed into the hole as the soft underbelly of Fafnir slammed over him.

Sigurd tried again. Gram cut deep into Fafnir's flesh.

There was another roar and more blood showered around him in gushing torrents. This time, Sigurd knew he'd hit the heart.

Fafnir collapsed to his side, his entire body twitching and spasming.

Sigurd pulled himself from the pit.

Despite being mortally wounded, Fafnir clung to life.

The dragon turned its fearsome yellow eyes to Sigurd. "You

who hid in a pit and slew me from below, history will remember this as a great battle, though you know it is not so. A coward slays Fafnir."

"A coward would not face mighty Fafnir, let alone slay him," Sigurd said, holding Gram at his side.

"Why do you come here?" Fafnir breathed, his eyes scanning their surroundings for someone else.

"I have come because my courage bid me to. I would test my strength against the well-known dragon and I have prevailed. You have been a fool to brag of your invincibility, inviting such a challenge."

"I do not believe you for a moment," Fafnir spat, his eyes bulging.

"Very well, I have come to claim the treasure you have so greedily stole from your kinsmen."

"Then you are a fool, for this treasure causes the death of all who own it."

"Were it so that I was an immortal man who lived forever, I would not claim a single coin from your horde. Yet, I remain mortal, and I will die, regardless of your gold's curse."

A poisonous cloud billowed from Fafnir's nostrils.

"Go now to Hel, Fafnir" Sigurd stated.

"Give me your name and your father's name, then I will depart the mortal world," Fafnir demanded.

"I am Sigurd, son of Sigmund. Slayer of Fafnir the dragon."

"I will see in you Hel before long," Fafnir said, a strange gleam in his eye. His enormous eyelids closed and the dragon passed from the world.

Sigurd sat in the dirt beside his fallen foe. His armour and clothes were soaked in the dragon's blood.

The crunching of leaves and sticks heralded the arrival of another.

"My Lord!" Regin gasped. "Such a feat will be remembered for all time. There has not been another who dare cross the path of Fafnir, let alone attempt to slay him. Yet here you stand, the mightiest of men beside the dead beast."

Anger flashed across Regin's face. "Yet you have killed my brother. A crime I had a part in, I know…"

Sigurd ignored Regin's sudden mood swing and began wiping his sword clean of the dragon's blood.

Regin frowned as he watched Sigurd.

"Without that sword I have so expertly crafted, you would have found your doom against Fafnir."

Sigurd spun to him and quickly retorted, "Let me tell you this, Regin, before you dare overstate your part in this feat. Anyone can craft a fine tool. Victory lies within a man's heart and soul, not his blade. I faced the dragon while you crept about in the shadows. You have no honour here."

Regin's face remained blank, yet his eyes lingered on the bleeding corpse of his brother.

"You will do me a favour, Sigurd," Regin said after a long moment of silence.

"Cut Fafnir's heart from his chest and build a fire. I would eat it."

Sigurd, frowning at this request, returned his clean sword to its scabbard and drew a long knife from his belt.

Three tiny wagtails fluttered about excitedly as Sigurd worked.

He began hacking through the dragon's broad chest and found its vast heart. It was as big as Sigurd's head.

While Regin sat in the shade of a large tree, Sigurd went to work fixing the heart to a spit over his raging fire.

He spun the monstrous wad of red muscle around and around, hoping for the blood to boil away. After fifteen minutes, Sigurd pressed his finger into the side of the heart to test it. He licked his finger, and something marvellous happened. As soon as the lingering blood from the heart's outer walls touched his tongue, he heard three unfamiliar voices emerge.

Sigurd scanned the area for the newcomers, though no new people could be found.

Suddenly, he realised it was the three wagtails who were speaking, as clearly as any person.

The first bird, sitting by its kin on a tall branch above Regin, excitedly stated, "There kneels Sigurd roasting the heart of Fafnir. Does he know that to eat the heart grants wisdom above all others?"

Sigurd looked from the branch to the heart, then to Regin.

The second wagtail chirped, "Regin will betray Sigurd. To have eyes is to see this plot. You cannot kill a brother, no matter how evil, and forget your family's honour."

The third bird hopped between the others and said, "Sigurd must kill Regin to prevent his treachery. Then he must ride to Fafnir's lair and claim his riches beyond measure."

"Lastly, Sigurd must go to Brynhild. On the mountain Hindarfjoll, behind a wall of flame, slumbers the cursed Valkyrie.

42

Only Sigurd has courage enough to wake her. Brynhild offers wisdom not even the heart of Fafnir does."

The second bird took the air, followed shortly by its fellows and said as it flew away, "Sigurd is not wise if he does not heed our advice. Neither Regin nor Sigurd can live together in this world from this point on. Regin knows this, does Sigurd?"

Sigurd watched the birds become small black specs in the distance.

He slowly turned the heart on its spit again, pondering the conversation he'd just heard. The blood of Fafnir had blessed him with the power to hear the language of birds, and apparently, the heart would grant him wisdom, with more to follow in the home of this Brynhild.

"I will not succumb to such a fate as to be slain by Regin," Sigurd muttered darkly.

Regin approached, looking impatient. Sigurd now noticed the dwarf's fingers resting on the hilt of his short sword.

In a move swift as the wind, Sigurd stood and drew Gram. In one fluid motion, he separated Regin's head from his body.

Both brothers lay dead, and Sigurd had prevented the bird's prophecy.

He returned to the roasting heart and carved a portion of it off. He bit through the tough leathery muscle. Boiling blood and other juices squirted into his mouth as he chewed. With a look of revulsion, Sigurd swallowed the flesh and felt illumination flash through his mind.

"Yes," he thought, *"I must go to Fafnir's lair and claim his treasure as my own."*

Mounting Greyfell, Sigurd began following the dragon's large tracks into the wilderness.

The three-toed markings of impressive size and fearsome visage carried a long way through the mud into the trees.

It wasn't long before he came across an impressive cave barred with iron gates. They were set on iron pillars dug deep into the earth.

This was the lair of Fafnir.

Fortunately, the gates were wide open and inside, Sigurd could see mounds of glittering treasure. Objects of all different shapes and sizes lay interspersed among piles of gold. Sigurd wondered just how he would carry it all.

Sigurd sat for a long time, stuffing what he could into large woven sacks. He built a sledge out of wood with the small hatchet on his belt when all the treasure was accounted for.

He heaved the sacks onto the sledge.

Greyfell eyed the heavy load nervously. No ordinary horse would be able to pull such a load, but Greyfell had divine lineage.

After a few words of encouragement, Sigurd mounted Greyfell and thrust his spurs into the horse's side. Greyfell whinnied and began moving with ease.

⟨HAPTER 6

BRYNHILD

They had not travelled far before they were forced to stop. A hulking figure cloaked in shadow, so large it consumed the entire road, was approaching.

At once, Sigurd knew what this creature was. It was a giant of Jotunheim.

The giant lowered his hood, revealing a strong beard and saucer-like eyes. He looked regal, dressed in finery beneath his cloak.

"I would speak with you, slayer of Fafnir," the giant said.

He didn't sound menacing or treacherous.

"My name is Skrymir, of the land Utgard."

"I know you from stories," Sigurd stated simply.

"Then you know that the land of Utgard is unfindable, even to the gods. That is why what I am about to ask is such an honour."

Sigurd raised his eyebrows, his face betraying his scepticism.

"Among the treasures you have just claimed are many magical rings. There is one I greatly desire, though I am not so presumptuous to assume you'd part with it freely," Skrymir said.

"What do you offer?" Sigurd asked.

"Among my collection are many treasures from many places. I would have you join me in travelling to Utgard and let you choose what your heart desires."

Sigurd considered the giant's request. His horse now carried more precious items than he could ever need. The risk of treachery from the giant was too high for an exchange that did not benefit him.

"The day has been long and I am weary. I will not travel to Utgard and do not wish to trade any of my newly acquired possessions," Sigurd stated absolutely.

"Disappointing," Skrymir said, looking sullen. The giant reached into his cloak and pulled a small glinting object from it. It was a horn shaped like a wolf.

"Take this horn. Press it to your lips and blow if you reconsider. It will take you to Utgard."

Skrymir held the horn delicately between his finger and thumb. Sigurd grasped it and nodded curtly to the giant.

"The horn will not sound unless there is silence in your ears. Find a place where all noise escapes you for the magic to work," Skrymir added. There was a colossal gust of wind and Skrymir vanished.

As soon as they began moving down the road, the encounter with the giant left Sigurd's mind. It would be a long time before he thought of it again.

Now his thoughts turned to the words of the birds. They had instructed Sigurd to go to the mountain Hindarfjoll. He knew this to be in the land of the Franks, though where it was he was not sure.

He took trackless paths and navigated the wildlands while pulling the sledge of treasures behind.

One night, he saw a bright glow on the horizon. He neglected sleep and made for the beacon with haste.

When the morning sun rose, Sigurd could see that atop a mountain sat a great wall of fire. He knew at last that he'd found Hindarfjoll.

He bade Greyfell onwards, and through craggy passes they climbed. When they reached the summit, Sigurd was surprised to find the inferno was so high that he could not see what it guarded.

"This must certainly be a mighty treasure to be guarded so well," Sigurd said to Greyfell.

He unfastened the sledge from his horse then circled the fire three times, unable to find a gap in the flames.

"This is where courage must take us and guide us through the fire, Greyfell," Sigurd said, stroking Greyfell's long black mane.

He kicked his spurs into Greyfell's side and they shot forward. Both horse and rider burst through the fire and onto the stony ground with an impressive leap.

Before Sigurd stood a tall tower made of stacked shields, with an unfamiliar banner at the top.

Behind the shield tower was a small building of white stone. It was only large enough to have a few rooms to it. It didn't look like a place where great wisdom could be found.

Sigurd drew Gram and dismounted Greyfell. He cautiously strode towards the odd structure and peered inside.

What he saw stunned him. A man was lying completely still on a long white table, with armour bound so tight around him it looked like it had merged into his flesh. On all sides he was surrounded by weapons of war.

Seeing no danger, Sigurd approached and removed the man's helmet.

It was no man at all but a woman. A woman of such breathtaking beauty Sigurd had to pause and observe her. She had a pale face and long golden hair. Her eyes were closed, though the grimace her mouth shaped showed discomfort.

At once, Sigurd began cutting her free of the suffocating armour that wrapped her.

When he pulled the mail-coat from her, she awoke.

"Who has freed me?" she asked, gazing into Sigurd's face. Her eyes were a mesmerizing silver.

"Sigurd, Sigmund's son," he replied.

Sigurd helped the woman to her feet.

"What is your name?"

"I am Brynhild, a Valkyrie."

Sigurd had suspected something of the divine about her. He knew Valkyries to be servants of Odin who guided the souls of the honourable dead to Valhalla. Often, they were born mortal women who were elevated by the god.

"How has a Valkyrie come to be in such a place?"

"There was a battle between two kings long ago. Odin had promised victory to one, though I favoured the other for reasons

I will not share. When my chosen slew the king, Odin pricked me with his thorn of sleep. He said that I would not know the battlefield again and would be wedded to a mortal man. I told the mighty god that I would never marry a man who knew the meaning of fear."

"That explains the wall of fire," Sigurd laughed.

Brynhild kept looking at him with her penetrating gaze.

"Are you a man of great renown?" she asked.

"I am Sigurd, slayer of Fafnir. I conquered the lands of the sons of Hunding. My courage serves me to the last."

"You will stay with me in this place," Brynhild said. "There is much I can teach. I will teach you to brew beer with magic that will grant fame, strength, gladness and healing to those who drink it.

"Then, I will teach you winning runes I learned from Tyr, God of War, to be written on weapons. Runes that will show treachery in personal dealings; I will show you how to write runes on drinking horns, that you may know if the drink is true. After this, you will learn birth runes so that the mother of your child will be safe. Write these on palms and around joints."

"A dwarf from Svartlfheim once tried to teach me rune magic, though I am ashamed to admit I was never any good at it."

"In my company, you will learn better, for I will see to it. Waves runes, speech runes, healing runes, thought runes and all others will make you a powerful warrior and powerful king."

"How do you know so much?"

"I have spent time in the company of gods well-versed in magic. If it would please you, I can teach you all that I know."

"I have heard from the speech of birds that there is great

wisdom to be found here. Is this wisdom the complete knowledge of runes?"

Brynhild smiled. "I know runes carved by Odin himself that grant wisdom beyond measure. But to know them, your knowledge must be complete in all other runes. The journey down this path is long and difficult and may cost much. Now, Sigurd, dragon slayer, you must choose which path you will walk. Remember, though you have a choice, your evil fate is already decided."

"Whether my fate is near or far, or evil as you claim, I will not flee. I will take your loving guidance for as long as I live."

On those words, Brynhild kissed Sigurd.

• • • • •

A long time passed while Sigurd and Brynhild lived atop that mountain. Both swore oaths to one another, pledging their eternal love.

As a token of his love, Sigurd gave Brynhild the greatest of the treasures of Fafnir, the ring Andvaranaut. The simple golden ring circled with faint runes sparkled on her finger. Using its power to create gold, Brynhild set to work modifying Sigurd's armour.

Soon, his helmet, greaves, gauntlets and chainmail all shone with a golden hue, emblazoned with the image of a dragon. Even his sword, Gram, now glowed with a golden hilt. Dressed in full battle attire, Sigurd no longer resembled a man. He looked like a god.

Brynhild, noticing the rune tattoos lining his left rib, decided to draw a dragon's image on his right arm. It looked precisely as

Sigurd had described Fafnir and was of the highest artistic skill.

During the days, Sigurd used his ability to speak with birds to aid his hunts. He befriended hawks who found prey with their keen eyes.

The love between Sigurd and Brynhild grew and grew, though both knew a time would come when Sigurd would leave.

Brynhild looked into Sigurd's future and saw that he would come to rule vast swathes of land, and he would soon have to go to a place where he would find allies.

Together, they had a daughter named Aslaug.

In this long period of peace, Sigurd honed his fighting skills even more. Brynhild, being a Valkyrie, had skills learned from the gods that she taught to Sigurd. His archery, swordsmanship and spear throwing became unmatched.

Sigurd also mastered the arts of courtesy and eloquence needed for a king.

One day, while hunting, Sigurd came across a band of travellers boasting of victories in battle.

"The sons of Gjuki are the finest of men. They have led us to victory after victory."

The loudest of the men wore a green tunic and brown hat. He looked battle-tested, with a prominent scar on his right cheek. The other two were younger and wrapped in the older man's words.

"But their kingdom is not so large, is it? Do you think they will take more land?" one of the boys asked excitedly.

The older man answered that there is no better pastime for men than war.

"Excuse me," Sigurd said, approaching the group. "From

where do you hail?"

"South of the Rhine. The Kingdom of Burgundy, just north of here."

"And who are these men you speak of?"

"King Gjuki, of course, and his three sons. Gunnar and Hogni are the best of leaders. The other, Guttorm, is just a boy."

The strangers eyed the gigantic Sigurd warily.

"And you say they are honourable men seeking to build an unmatched kingdom?"

"Yes. A man of your size and stature would fair well in battle and earn great honour."

This was the sign Sigurd had been waiting for. At last, he had a destination.

When Sigurd returned to Brynhild that night, she looked as if she already knew his words before he spoke them.

"I will take our daughter to my father, Budli. He is a powerful king in his own right. Then, when the time is right, I know you will return to this place and ride through the flames again to take me as your wife. I would have no other man."

"I shall marry you, or no other woman," Sigurd swore.

The evening light, flickering through the window, caught Andvaranaut in its dying rays as the pair embraced.

That morning, dressed in his glorious golden attire, Sigurd mounted Greyfell and began his journey north.

⟨HAPTER 7

SIGURD MARRIES

Not only did King Gjuki have three sons, but he also had a daughter. Within his kingdom, none were fairer than Princess Gudrun. With chestnut hair and deep brown eyes, she stirred the affections of suitors far and wide. Not only was she beautiful, but she was kind. She carried herself with all the grace and nobility a highborn woman should.

King Gjuki was a powerful man who'd chosen a wife gifted with magic. Some called Queen Grimhild a witch, though only in secretive mutterings. The gifts in her blood flowed down into her daughter, who occasionally had prophetic dreams.

One night, while Gudrun was fast asleep, she was encompassed by a vision of particular clarity.

She stood alone in the forest. A golden falcon swooped down and nestled itself in her arms. She loved this falcon more than anything in the world. It shined brighter and better than all things.

Her three brothers approached from a dark path. Shadows had fallen across their faces. They all had daggers in their hands, and when they drew near, they stabbed the golden falcon to death. Just behind them stood a woman that Gudrun did not know. As the bird died, the strange woman laughed joyously and wailed in anguish.

Gudrun woke with a start, perplexed as to the meaning of it.

She was disappointed to find that she had the same dream the next night, though this time the falcon was a majestic stag.

Some nights the dream changed. Instead of the bright falcon, a fat smelly bird that Gudrun did not recognise landed in her arms. She hated this bird immensely.

Through the days, as she weaved intricate tapestries, she pondered the meaning of these dreams. Was the golden falcon a man that she would love above all others? And if so, who was he?

Gudrun certainly didn't know of any such man now.

• • • • •

There came a day when a great stir ran through Gjuki's hall. One of the king's men had arrived in a fluster to announce the news. Apparently, a stranger had come to town, a stranger draped in golden armour who looked like a god.

Draped in his glorious armour and riding the most magnificent stallion anyone had ever seen, Sigurd came to the Kingdom of Burgundy.

In the time that had passed, the whole world had learned of his defeat of Fafnir.

The common folk recognised that this was Sigurd, son of Sigmund, killer of the five kings and dragon-slayer.

When word reached Gjuki of this renowned hero's arrival, he summoned Sigurd at once.

"Your reputation proceeds you, Sigurd of the Volsung line," Gjuki said.

"As does yours," Sigurd replied.

"Let me introduce my sons, Gunnar and Hogni."

Two young men approached and greeted Sigurd enthusiastically. Both were tall (though falling far short of Sigurd) and handsome. They looked like they could swing swords furiously but also had faces for diplomacy.

"The youngest, Guttorm, is too young to swing a blade," Gjuki said.

"Your accomplishments are well known in these lands. Word of your victories has carried far."

"You honour us," Gunnar said.

"Would you do us yet a further honour and ride with us tomorrow?" Hogni asked.

"It is why I am here," Sigurd smiled.

They began drinking and feasting. Through the corner of Sigurd's eye, he saw a beautiful woman staring at him from behind a pillar. She ducked away nervously when he turned his head towards her.

"Who is that?" Sigurd asked.

"Our sister, Gudrun," Gunnar laughed. "It seems she has

eyes for dragon-slayers."

"Her glance falls in the wrong direction, for I am promised to another."

Gunnar looked at him curiously.

"Not far from here lives a woman in a house surrounded by flame. She is the greatest of women and will be my wife in time."

"What is her name?" Gunnar asked.

"Brynhild."

"She must truly be quite the woman to have captured your attention," a new voice said.

A woman with a pointed face and small eyes approached. She smiled warmly.

"Queen Grimhild," Sigurd said, standing and bowing.

Grimhild wore a long black dress beneath an emerald cloak. Her fingers glittered with exotic jewels attached to elaborate rings. Around her neck sat a necklace of diamonds.

"There is no need for that," Grimhild said. "It is a shame you have sworn oaths to another. It would be good luck for you to join this family through marriage. Then the three of you would be brothers fighting together."

"Brotherhood can be formed in war as equally as in marriage," Sigurd said. "Though I am flattered nonetheless."

"Your horse has been stabled and the vast amounts of wealth you brought, treasures and weapons of war like I have never seen, are under guard in our treasury."

Grimhild moved away but spent the rest of the evening watching Sigurd intently.

• • • • •

That morning, Sigurd did indeed go riding with Gunnar and Hogni. The three men came across a band of outlaws, more than twenty strong. Thanks to their combined skill and Sigurd's leadership, they were the only ones who left that place alive.

Sigurd came to stay for a long while. Alongside Gunnar and Hogni, he commanded Gjuki's army to many victories.

Sigurd often spoke with loving admiration of Brynhild. Whenever Grimhild was around, she was quick to change the subject. Sigurd never noticed her reluctance to talk of the Valkyrie.

One night, during a celebratory feast, Grimhild again approached Sigurd. She offered him a drinking horn full of mead.

"Never have our lands been larger or our army stronger. Gjuki treats you as if you are his own blood, and so do I. Let us drink to shared victories."

Sigurd drained his horn in a single gulp. A warm feeling washed over him, and his mind went temporarily blank. He snapped himself out of it, feeling a little dazed, and continued feasting.

Grimhild smiled as she walked away. Only she knew that Sigurd had forgotten something of great importance. He had forgotten Brynhild.

• • • • •

In the following months, Sigurd came to notice that Gudrun was indeed beautiful and noble. He wondered how he hadn't seen it before. He didn't dare approach the king's daughter for fear of causing offence, but that didn't stop them from going on long walks together. They discussed philosophy and meaning, and Sigurd found himself wrapped in her company.

Sigurd, Gunnar, and Hogni led armies in campaigns against foreign kings for the next two and half years. They were always victorious and amassed wealth beyond measure.

After speaking with his father and mother, Gunnar approached Sigurd while he tended to Greyfell in the stables.

"Sigurd, it is time we discussed something."

Sigurd looked at him curiously.

"The joy you have brought us cannot be overstated. I would have you join our family in more than just words. It is not easy for a father to give away his daughter, but my father wishes you to marry Gudrun. She also believes there is no finer man for her to wed. Further to this, Hogni and I will swear oaths of blood-brotherhood to you. We will be as if we came from the same father. What say you?"

"I am honoured, and of course, I accept."

"That is not all. You will join us as king. This kingdom is yours as much as it is mine now. All hail King Sigurd," he winked.

There was a celebration that lasted for days. Sigurd married Gudrun, and as a wedding present, he gave her part of Fafnir's heart to eat. She gained wisdom from it but also became less kind.

Everything was as it should be in Sigurd's life. Now complete, he turned his attention to his brothers, particularly Gunnar.

He needed a wife.

Shortly after Sigurd's son, Sigmund (named after his father) was born to Gudrun, Grimhild approached Sigurd and Gunnar.

"It is time, Gunnar, for you to go and woo Brynhild the Valkyrie. The two of you are a perfect match. Sigurd will ride with you."

Gunnar looked at Sigurd for advice.

"This is a good plan. I have heard legends of her beauty and wisdom."

Gunnar prepared his most spectacular armour set and rode with Sigurd to Hindarfjoll. They crossed the craggy passes and navigated steep paths, which seemed very familiar to Sigurd.

At last, they were confronted with the tall wall of flames that encircled Brynhild's home.

Gunnar tried to ride his horse through the fire, but the beast wouldn't do it.

Sigurd offered him Greyfell, but Greyfell would not listen to any other rider's commands. Not even on Sigurd's request would Greyfell carry Gunnar through the fire.

"Do not let your courage fail you," Sigurd said. "Command your horse and steel your nerve. You can get through the fire."

"I am not sure I can," Gunnar sighed. "Only a man such as yourself can leap those flames. Here is what you will do. We will change clothes. You will pass the test and tell Brynhild that you are me and that I am here to have her hand in marriage. My helmet is full-faced, so she won't know. When you leave her home, go ahead of her down the mountain. I will be waiting. We will trade clothes, and I will take Brynhild back by myself. I would like the chance to get to know her."

"It would sit more comfortably with me if you were just to leap the flames yourself. But you are my brother and I will not deny your request," Sigurd said.

Wearing Gunnar's glittering armour, he mounted Gunnar's horse.

Gunnar thrust a ring into Sigurd's hand. "Take the ring from her finger and give her this one instead."

Sigurd agreed and charged through the fire.

The earth shook and the flames reached for the heavens as he crossed it.

He approached the white stone building and knocked on the door. Sigurd noticed that the roof was coated with gold, though he had no idea how it was possible.

Brynhild emerged, looking hopeful. It was like she was expecting someone.

"Name yourself," she demanded.

"Gunnar, son of Gjuki, King of Burgundy. I have come for your hand in marriage."

Sigurd made sure to alter his voice slightly. He couldn't help but notice that Brynhild looked crestfallen.

"If you have leapt through the flames, you have passed the test. Though, you should know I have sworn oaths to another. I fear he is gone, though, for he has not returned to me in a long time…"

"You are as beautiful as the legends describe. Come with me to my father's hall. I promise that I will be a good husband and good man to you."

"I will only marry a man who will swear to kill any other who seeks my hand."

"Remember your own oath that you would marry the man

with the courage to ride through the fire."

Brynhild understood that this man was indeed a great king from these words.

"I will give you this ring in exchange for the one on your finger. A symbol of new promises made."

Brynhild gave the small golden ring to Sigurd, who instantly recognised it. This was Andvaranaut, part of Fafnir's treasure. Though how Brynhild had ended up with it, he had no idea.

Brynhild went to pack her things as the fire around her home burnt out.

Sigurd ducked away, throwing the armour off and jumping onto Greyfell. He felt guilty for his part in this deception, though he wasn't sure why.

He rode back towards his own wife, Gudrun, as fast as the wind.

• • • • •

Later that week, when Gunnar arrived with Brynhild, Sigurd couldn't help but notice the shock, horror and hurt that crossed her face when she laid eyes on him. Yet, she greeted him warmly.

"I am surprised, Sigurd. I thought you would be the only one with the daring to ride through my ring of fire, yet it turns out there was another."

At these words, memory came flooding back to Sigurd. He remembered the oaths and his daughter, Aslaug. For a moment, he was stunned and saddened. He couldn't find the words to say to Brynhild at that moment, though in his mind, they were of loss and regret.

Brynhild moved on to be greeted by more of Gjuki's family.

Sigurd at once confided everything he remembered to Gudrun.

"My mother has fooled you with a potion. I did not know of this plot, yet I remain joyous that everything has worked out as it should," she said simply.

"You are a good wife to me. Here, I will give you Andvaranaut to place on your finger. This is the most prized item of Fafnir's treasure. I hope it serves you well."

Sigurd slipped the cursed ring onto Gudrun's finger.

Brynhild adjusted to life in Gjuki's hall well. However, despite the man's continual best efforts to impress her, she didn't seem entirely fond of Gunnar.

One day both Gudrun and Brynhild headed to the river to bathe. When they reached the bank, Brynhild moved slightly further upstream than Gudrun.

"Why do you move so far away from me?" Gudrun asked playfully.

Brynhild scoffed and responded in a tone that implied Gudrun was foolish for asking.

"Surely you do not think us equals? It is only right that we do not bathe in the same spot."

"Oh, and which one of us do you think is greater?" Gudrun retorted, immediately firing up.

"Well, my husband rode through a ring of fire to claim me. He is the true king of these lands and far more accomplished than yours."

Gudrun marched up to Brynhild. "I'll have you know that none are more accomplished than Sigurd, a fact you well know. It was he who slew the dragon Fafnir. It was he who first rode through the ring of fire and it was he who became your first lover!"

"Then the question becomes this: what is a woman like you doing with Sigurd? Is it more treachery from your witch-mother?"

"I'll have you know that none have ever questioned that Sigurd and I are equals!" Gudrun shouted. "I am sorry that Sigurd broke his oaths to you, but he is my husband now. Try to restrain your jealousy so that it doesn't flow from your mouth in foolish ways."

"Sigurd would be my husband were it not for spells and evil tricks. Yet, I am not concerned, for Gunnar matches him in courage."

"Gunnar does not remotely possess the courage of Sigurd! Look at this ring on my finger and see for yourself!"

Gudrun showed Brynhild Andvaranaut.

Her face fell.

"How did you come to possess that ring?" she asked quietly.

"It was not Gunnar who rode through fire! It was not Gunnar who took that ring from you and asked you to be his wife. Sigurd did it on his behalf!"

Brynhild's face fell, and Gudrun knew she had said too much.

Before she could say anything else, Brynhild ran away.

Gudrun felt an ill omen floating in the air around her. Brynhild was a fierce woman and would not take the news of this treachery well.

Gudrun gathered up her things and made for the hall, where she bumped into Sigurd.

"Sigurd, do you remember when you told me of the giant who approached you on the path from Fafnir's lair?" she asked quickly.

"Of course..." Sigurd began.

"I want you to go to Utgard. You still have the horn he gave you, right?"

"I do, yes. What has brought this about?"

"Find me a foreign treasure worthy of your queen."

"Very well," Sigurd said blankly, looking very suspicious. "But when I return, I hope you will be honest with me as to why you want me gone."

Gudrun paused, looking very nervous.

"I have told Brynhild the truth of your deception with Gunnar. I didn't mean to, I got angry. I think it is best if you leave for a short time if you wish to keep on living," she blurted out.

Sigurd understood.

"This is an unfortunate thing. Perhaps there is wisdom in your fear. Regardless, I should remove myself while Gunnar and Brynhild come to an understanding."

"Will you forgive my foolishness? The heart of Fafnir was meant to make me wise. It seems it has only made me cruel," Gudrun said.

"You are always forgiven," Sigurd said, pulling his wife close. "I will get Gram and ready Greyfell to ride."

"Are you sure this idea is safe?" Gudrun asked.

"Those long years ago, when I met the giant, he seemed

genuine in his request. And if he is not, soon I will be called giant-slayer and dragon-slayer."

Gudrun chuckled, wiping her eyes.

Sigurd went to their chambers and fetched the small wolf-shaped horn from deep within a chest of his most guarded possessions. He remembered the giant had said he must only hear silence to travel to Utgard. He also recalled that the giant had wanted a ring from Fafnir's treasure horde.

Sigurd went to his treasury and gathered every ring, anklet and armband he could find. Soon, his arms were wreathed in glittering jewels, making Sigurd feel foolish.

Yet, a youthful glimmer of excitement rose in his chest. It had been some time since Sigurd had been on a proper adventure.

Sigurd bade farewell to his son, kissing him tenderly on the head.

He then bade fond farewells to Gudrun, Gunnar and Hogni. He told Gunnar that Brynhild was a good woman and that she would see his worth in time.

Mounting Greyfell, he rode into the night.

⟨HAPTER 8

UTGARD

Finding a place that was not pierced with the noise of wind or birds turned out to be surprisingly tricky.

It took days of travel, which was made all the more difficult as he had no clear destination in mind.

When he came to the edge of a dark forest, he thought that within its confines might be a place where the trees are so thick that not even the wind could pass.

Deeper and deeper he travelled into the unknown. The shadows of tall trees darkened his path and strange bird calls gave the forest an air of dread. Even Greyfell, who'd never had a day without courage, seemed nervous.

He came into a clearing ringed with gnarled trees. Their long branches and wrinkled bark showed their tremendous age. There was no movement. Not even the wind whistled in this place.

Hastily, Sigurd reached for the horn attached to his belt and pressed it to his lips. No sounds emerged when he blew, yet Sigurd felt its effects instantly. The dead leaves beneath him were blown away as a series of sparks began drawing dark brown lines on the forest floor.

The outer circle, of what appeared to be a layered, complex image that was quite wide, shaped itself into being. Sigurd could've fit himself within its circumference several times over.

With a gasp that shattered the eerie stillness of the forest, Sigurd was hoisted into the air. He floated for a moment, lost for words. Part of him wondered if he'd fallen into a trap set by the giant he'd met all those years ago.

Rainbow light began bursting in ribbons from the circle below him, flickering upwards and licking his boots. Sigurd vaguely recognised this light from descriptions by travellers from the far north, who said dancing greens and purples moved across the night sky.

There was a rushing of air and a sensation like he was falling through glass, then the world was inverted.

Sigurd came plummeting down, crashing hard onto his back.

He quickly stood, drawing Gram in fear of an attack. He looked left to right in panic. When nothing came for him, he soaked in his new surroundings.

He'd moved from the dark forest to somewhere wholly foreign.

Around Sigurd was an endless sea of tall green grass below a blank blue sky. The only jarring object that broke its sameness was a large grey castle, not too far away.

Sigurd figured that this could only be one place, the mythical Utgard. He looked down to see that none of the enchanted rings or armbands had fallen from him. Satisfied he hadn't lost any of the trinkets, he sheathed Gram and marched towards the castle.

There wasn't an insect to be heard here. Not even the most meagre buzzing fly or scurrying ant could be seen.

The castle was otherworldly. Each brick shimmered in the radiant sun. Several tall towers were topped with bulbous blue domes of the most magnificent sapphire. The light intensified as it hit them and showered the surrounding walls in a cascade of blue.

The upper ramparts and balconies that lined the outer structure's various levels were immaculate. Sigurd knew through sight alone that they'd never seen war or conflict.

After a short while, Sigurd came into a grey courtyard lined with tall pillars. Atop each sat a leering gargoyle, so expertly carved they threatened to come to life at any moment.

Behind the rows of pillars was a black door, too large for a man but perfectly suited for a giant.

The door creaked open as if anticipating his arrival. Sigurd rested his hand on Gram's hilt as he stepped into the hall.

To his right was a spiralling stair that rose to the second floor landing. He walked past long wooden tables on his left that were lined with red and gold cloth. It was made of the softest velvet he'd ever touched.

The hall was completely deserted yet didn't look abandoned. He ran his hand along the high-backed chairs that were scattered by the tables in a disordered fashion, noting the absence of dust. They'd been recently used.

About halfway along the hall was a strange alcove in the wall. It looked like a giant sky-blue mural was being built in the shape of a tall door but was only half-finished. Sigurd stared at it and sensed strong magic, then decided to give it a wide berth.

Sigurd had never seen a place quite like this in all his travels. It was from a time older than his, a time when the gods adventured more frequently through the realms of men and giants.

At the end of the hall was a throne fit for a giant. It was stone and decorated with glowing magical runes and strange hieroglyphs. At once, Sigurd understood that the throne was designed to amplify its sitter's power.

"Hello?" Sigurd called. His voice echoed off the high ceiling.

A large wooden door swung open near the throne. Inside, Sigurd peeked a dining hall with gigantic tables and seats.

From the door, came a figure Sigurd remembered from his youth, the giant Skrymir.

He looked shocked to see Sigurd standing there.

The giant even rubbed his eyes in disbelief.

Skrymir wore a long fur robe of deep maroon with white sleeves and jewels embedded down its centre. On his head, sat a simple golden crown, and his large hands were heavily decorated with jewellery. It would've been impressive if Sigurd's own hands weren't equally covered.

"Sigurd of the Volsung line!" Skrymir boomed. "I never thought you would come! Watched your adventures from afar, I have. What a warrior! What a fighter!"

Sigurd felt rather humbled by the giant's flattering words.

"You honour me," Sigurd mumbled, bowing low.

"The honour is mine!" Skrymir bellowed.

He moved to his throne and peered at the man before him.

"Long ago, you asked for an item of Fafnir's treasure. I denied you then, though I remember you said it was a ring. I have brought every ring with me, save the infamous Andvaranaut, which I claim as my own."

Skrymir looked on greedily as Sigurd plucked the rings and bands from his arms and held them before the giant.

"Pass me the golden ring embedded with blue opals," Skrymir said, and Sigurd did so.

Astonishingly, as soon as the object hit the giant's palm, it grew in size.

"Yes…" murmured Skrymir.

"I have never seen that particular ring looked at as more than an object of beauty," Sigurd frowned.

"Long ago, I heard rumours that a lesser ring of power in Andvari's treasure could strengthen distant magics. I often feel pulled to places far away, though I don't understand it. This ring will help me."

"Then you may have it as a gift," Sigurd said simply. "My wealth is so great I have no need for one extra ring."

"No, a deal was offered, so a deal must be made. I will show you my collection of treasures, and you will choose an item of equal value."

Another figure walked in from the open side door. He was not a giant, nor was he a man. Like the gargoyles earlier, this looked like a statue of a person had come to life. He was perfect in his design, though he had empty eyes. The newcomer was hard to look at it, as if the air warped and the light twisted in odd ways in his presence.

"A mortal champion," the stranger spoke. His voice and accent were unlike anything Sigurd had ever heard.

"Prometheus, this is Sigurd. The greatest living warrior north of the Mediterranean! Perhaps, in the world! We will see…"

Other figures began filtering into the great hall.

Sigurd noticed dwarves, much like Regin, and elves of varying kinds. There were odder creatures too. A thin brown-skinned man wearing a white knee-length loincloth and magnificent gold and sapphire armbands appeared among the crowd. Where his head should've been sat the head of a green long-billed bird.

The bird-man scribbled on an extended roll of parchment, paying Sigurd no attention.

Sigurd knew that this being was a god, but unlike any god he'd seen.

Skrymir watched Sigurd curiously.

"I'm sure you are familiar with the Aesir. Thor, Odin, Loki and their like. I am familiar with them too," Skrymir said darkly. "Ever since Thor's visit, I have made Utgard a welcome escape for many different gods. We will leave this hall, as you seem to have drawn a crowd."

Sigurd bowed again as Skrymir stood. The giant clapped his hands and the castle moved around them. In the time it took to blink, Sigurd was somewhere new. His stomach churned violently from the process.

He looked through a window and saw he was now high up

in Utgard.

The corridor was well lit with torches and lined with tapestries. Skrymir directed Sigurd towards a door with no handle.

"In here, see my treasures. I will leave you to look while I prepare. When you have found something you desire, simply clap your hands and the castle will take you back down."

Skrymir then, without warning, disappeared.

"Prepare what?" Sigurd asked the spot where Skrymir had just been.

Feeling uneasy and gripping the hilt of Gram ever tighter, Sigurd made for the handle-less door.

It swung open for him, and he entered a world of wonders.

On every wall were mounts holding magnificent weapons. Along the floor were display cases holding objects that radiated power.

Sigurd had to rub his eyes. Most of it was so foreign he didn't know where to begin. Blazing light shined from the magical items, filling the room with a rainbow of colour.

He walked the length of the long room and found stairs going up and down. An entire wing of the castle was devoted to the giant's treasure horde.

A white arched window sat against the back wall, and Sigurd looked out of it to see something even more astonishing.

Enclosures of various sizes holding all sorts of fantastical creatures were occupying the grasslands behind the castle. Sigurd saw a troll, an enormous fire-breathing lion, and human-headed animals lazily sunning themselves. He deduced that the giant collected both the living and the inanimate.

Sigurd had truly stepped out of his life and into a mythical story.

This realisation made him anxious to pick an object at random and get out of here. What if the giant collected people too? Indeed King Sigurd, slayer of Fafnir, was a prize beyond all others.

"Do not fear that fate," a voice said.

Sigurd raised Gram in alarm and spun on the spot. It was the strange stone man he'd seen in the entry hall.

"My name is Prometheus," he said curtly.

"Sigurd."

"I thought I might help you make sense of what Skrymir keeps in here. Some relics come from your lands. Some from mine."

Prometheus pointed to a silver zig-zag shape mounted to the wall. It looked like a metal recreation of a lightning bolt.

"I also offer a friendly warning. Skrymir believes you to be the perfect mortal champion of Utgard. He will offer you a place here."

"And what does being his champion mean?"

"You would have to give up your earthly possessions and ties to mortality. In ever-still Utgard you would linger, a defender against threats to Skrymir's realm."

"I do not wish this for myself. I have a young family and a kingdom."

"Understandable," Prometheus said.

"I already have wealth and many fine objects," Sigurd said. "I would appreciate your guidance for an item that gives me what I don't already have."

Prometheus walked down the long room and stood by a

glass case. Sigurd approached, being careful not to look at the odd man directly.

"Take the small white cube from the glass."

Sigurd frowned, as he could not see a way to open the case, let alone grasp the object. He pressed his hand against the glass and was astonished to see it melt.

He gripped the cube and quickly withdrew his hand.

"What is it?" Sigurd asked.

"I sense that you have a powerful bond with your steed. A bond forged in war. Split this cube in half, then eat one side of it. Feed the other to your horse. While you live, your horse will be tied to life. Old age and injury will not stop him as long as you draw breath."

"If I were to die, would Greyfell too?"

"No, the spell only works with life, not death. However, if you were dead, and so was Greyfell, and you found a way to come back, I suspect he would too."

"This truly is a useful gift. You have my thanks."

Sigurd studied the small cube closely. It was devoid of markings or instructions, yet its power was unique.

"Don't thank me, thank the Lord of Utgard."

Prometheus clapped his hands, and they both zoomed back into the great hall.

Skrymir was sitting on his throne.

"An interesting choice," he said, eyeing the cube clutched in Sigurd's hand. "Of course, very few animals would bare me as a rider. I have no need for it; take it with my good grace."

"Thank you for the gift, Lord Skrymir."

"You are most welcome, King Sigurd. Now, I have a request to ask of you. Your fighting prowess is well known, even here. Among the citizens of Utgard are many skilled warriors. I would have you fight each one to see if the legends of Sigurd are true."

Pride and honour compelled Sigurd to answer before any consideration had taken place.

"I will fight your champions."

A general cheer went up from all the creatures in the hall.

"Then let's begin," Skrymir grinned. "While I'd like to make this a more formal affair, I'm afraid you caught me at a busy time. We will see your skill in the time we have.

There was a rushing of air, and Sigurd moved again. He appeared beneath the bright blue sky in a large arena walled by high spectator seats. The ground was entirely comprised of a red mushy material Sigurd didn't recognise.

Skrymir's voice, magically magnified, boomed across the arena, announcing that each warrior would face Sigurd, one after another.

Sigurd held Gram before him and readied himself.

He shook his legs and cracked his neck, giving the sword a few test waves.

As the giant had said, warrior after warrior came at Sigurd. Some used magic and others used brute strength to cut him down, but all fell against his blade.

It was different for Sigurd, fighting non-human foes. The elves were nimble and the sturdy dwarves could take a beating before they fell.

The grotesque spectacle of it made Sigurd feel alive. The

roars and groans of the crowd flowed through him as he landed killing blow after killing blow.

When seven challengers had fallen and a slick sheen of blood coated Gram, the eighth appeared.

Sigurd could tell this was no mortal. This person was ethereal, like he was made of grey smoke. He was muscular and bearded, wielding a square hammer with a handle that was slightly too short.

It was a ghostly recreation of the God Thor that Skrymir's magic had brought to life. Sigurd knew this to be the giant's true test.

The ghost-Thor bellowed, earning a cheer from the crowd. He ran at Sigurd, who dodged a hammer strike but couldn't avoid the hail of lightning from the sky. His muscles seized up in excruciating pain as the electricity flowed through him. Even in his agony, Sigurd noticed the electricity flowed towards his sword more than his body.

Gritting his teeth, Sigurd pushed himself up while the ghostly Thor laughed. His voice sounded like clapping thunder.

Ghost-Thor spun his hammer and shot a bolt of lightning right at Sigurd.

He threw himself to the side, avoiding the blast by millimetres. His hair stood on its ends.

Sigurd ran at Thor, holding Gram out in front. If he didn't control the fight, the ghost would continue to strike him down again and again with electricity.

He was ready for it this time.

When Thor's hammer's next blast of lightning sparked into

life, Sigurd planted Gram into the ground and dived to the side.

Gram acted as a lightning rod, allowing Sigurd to jump forward.

His careening body came to a stop near Thor's boot.

He pulled a long-curved knife from his belt and thrust it straight into the ghostly foot.

When the ethereal grey god moved to bring his hammer down, Sigurd planted a second knife in his throat.

The ghost exploded into crackling mist, and the crowd cheered. Skrymir roared his approval.

Sigurd barely had a moment to compose himself before he was again transported across space.

"A spectacular show," Skrymir grinned broadly.

Sigurd wiped the sweat from his brow and pushed his long hair away from his face.

"I have played your game and shown my worth. I'd like to return to my home now."

"It shall be done. But first, consider this. Become my champion and stay in Utgard. I can teach you magic beyond anything in the mortal world."

"I have much to live for in Midgard. I regret to say that I cannot become your champion. Though in time, it could become an option."

Skrymir looked sorrowful.

"Worth a try," he mumbled. "Keep the horn, but put it somewhere safe. Use it, should you reconsider."

Sigurd nodded formally at Skrymir, then at Prometheus.

The world inverted and shattered like glass again, and Sigurd was back in the dark forest.

He looked down at his hands. Had that all been a bizarre dream? He saw the dark head of Greyfell in the nearby trees.

"Come here, Greyfell. Let us bind ourselves to one another so that I will always have you as my horse while I live."

Sigurd pulled the white cube from his pocket. His knife cut it into two even pieces. He put one in Greyfell's mouth and swallowed the other. It was sour and rubbery.

Still, if it worked, it was worth the trouble.

Before heading back home to face the marital problems of Brynhild and Gunnar, he took a detour to Gnitaheath.

· · · · ·

The place where he'd killed Fafnir had changed over the years. A landslide had covered the bones of Fafnir completely. Some of the ruined buildings could still be seen poking through the dirt. Soon this area would be lost to history. The land was trying to erase the terrible memory of the dragon.

It was here that Sigurd decided to bury the horn, as it was a place he could never forget.

Then, with the sun at his back, he turned in the direction of Gjuki's hall, and the problems he couldn't avoid forever.

⟨HAPTER 9

TREACHERY AND DEATH

Upon his return, Sigurd was surprised to find that Gudrun was not interested in his tale of Utgard and Skyrmir. In fact, she was beside herself with worry about Brynhild.

Gudrun said that Brynhild had become despondent, not caring for food or drink. Apparently, she was seldom seen out of her chambers.

Even more worrying was the news that Brynhild had apparently attacked Gunnar in her rage, causing Hogni to bind her in chains. Sigurd was relieved to hear that Gunnar had immediately ordered her free.

Gudrun had tried in vain to repair their relationship, to no avail. And now Brynhild would not speak to anyone, not even her husband.

Sigurd valued Gunnar's friendship and desperately didn't want to involve himself in the man's marital problems. Nonetheless, it now seemed time that he must go and speak to Brynhild.

The very afternoon of his arrival, he strode up to Brynhild's room and knocked on her door.

There was no answer.

Sigurd forced it open and found Brynhild lying still, pretending to sleep.

Sigurd pulled the sheets away from her and said, "Get up and stop this misery that consumes you. You have much to be joyful for. Your husband is a good man and a good king, and it is wrong of you to live in regret for what should have been."

Brynhild looked at Sigurd with tears in her eyes.

"It is not Gunnar who slew the dragon Fafnir. It is not Gunnar who rode through the flames to wake me. It is not Gunnar who swore oaths of undying love to me. I hate that man! Though I pretend not to. You ought to be my husband, Sigurd."

"Do you not think that I was filled with regret and horror when the spell broke? All memory of private words spoken flooded back to me in the rush of the most powerful river. Yet it does no one any good to dwell in the past. If you were to give Gunnar a chance, you would see that he is a fine man and good husband to you."

"You only speak out of guilt," Brynhild sobbed. "I swore to marry the man who rode through the flames, words which are now robbed of meaning by you. I would rather die than face another day of this life."

"Do not bring voice to such evils, Brynhild. It is unbecoming of you."

"How dare you say what is unbecoming of me! You who

broke your oath! You who tricked me! I would say no more to you!"

She got to her feet and pushed Sigurd out of the room, slamming the door behind him.

Sigurd returned to Gudrun, who was waiting anxiously in the great hall.

"How did it go? Did you bring sense back to her?" she asked quietly.

"Not well. But I hope time and the ever-constant breaking of new days will dull the wound Brynhild feels in her heart."

Gudrun looked at Sigurd nervously and said, "I am worried for us."

"Do not be. Come, let us go somewhere in the sun and I will tell you tales of Utgard and giants."

The pair strode off to enjoy the rest of the day together. It was a difficult task, with the storm clouds of worry hanging high overhead.

• • • • •

Later that night, when Gunnar returned to his chambers, he found Brynhild in utter despair. He hastened to her side and asked, "What has happened?"

"Sigurd came to my chamber," Brynhild sobbed. "And here he took advantage of me, breaking all oaths of brotherhood sworn to you."

"I can hardly believe it," Gunnar said in shock. "Sigurd has always been an honourable man."

"You would believe in Sigurd's honour over the words of your own wife?" Brynhild screeched, looking completely deranged.

81

Gunnar was taken aback, and any response left him.

"If you do not kill Sigurd, I will leave you," Brynhild said quietly, every word pulsing with venom.

A silence hung in the air between them.

"You had no courage to ride through the fire and no courage now," Brynhild spat.

These words stirred a wave of terrible anger in Gunnar.

"I am not the small man you think me to be!"

"Then you will kill Sigurd and his son."

"I do not know why you spurn the love I have for you," Gunnar said. "You are the greatest of all women, and I would rather die than lose you. Yet your mind only ever lingers on Sigurd."

Brynhild glared at him.

"You will never touch me again, nor will I lay in your bed while Sigurd lives."

Gunnar frowned, then strode from the room to collect his thoughts.

After a short time, he sought out Hogni, who looked aghast when Gunnar revealed what he had to do.

"You cannot do this. To break such an oath will have terrible unforeseeable consequences. You know Brynhild hates Sigurd for old promises broken. To take her word on this is a fool's decision."

"She is my wife!" Gunnar yelled.

Hogni fell silent.

"Think about it, brother; with Sigurd dead, the entire kingdom will be ours. All of these lands and his wealth to share between us."

"Never again will we have such a brother-in-law as Sigurd.

What he has done for us cannot be measured and to break our oaths with violence will bring shame and harm upon us."

"I have made my decision. This is the way it must be."

"Brynhild spews poison like the dragon Fafnir, clouding your mind to reason. Regardless, you cannot break your oath."

"Nor can you. There is one who can attack Sigurd, though. Our youngest brother, Guttorm, must see this task done."

Hogni grimaced. Seeing there was nothing he could say to prevent the coming catastrophe, he nodded.

There was no time to waste. Sigurd's death had to come quickly.

The two brothers began gathering ingredients to brew into a stew, a stew with specific malicious intent invented by their witch-mother Grimhild.

"A terrible deed this will be, brother. History will remember us poorly for the events of this night," Hogni, once again, cautioned his brother.

Gunnar said nothing. His purpose was clear.

The brothers began work preparing the stew. In a bubbling pot, they mixed snake's meat, wolf's meat, beer, and other things.

When at last the malevolent mix was finished, Guttorm was summoned.

In the quiet mead hall, the youngest of them drank deep of the enchanted stew, and a change came over him.

Fire glowed in his eyes and his temple pulsed with sweat.

"I will commit this murder in your honour, brothers," Guttorm said aggressively. His fringe flopped forward over his face, making the boy look wild and unhinged.

He began frantically pacing back and forth.

"The honour is yours to kill a man such as Sigurd who has wronged us so," Gunnar said. His voice was entirely devoid of emotion.

Gunnar presented Guttorm with a sword. It was of a simple make, and the hall's fire was reflected in its dull gleam.

The moon still hung high on the black canvas of night as Guttorm approached Sigurd's bed.

The door creaked open, and Guttorm snuck inside. He looked down at the sleeping king and was overcome with such terrible fear and apprehension that he fled the room in a panic.

Outside the room, Guttorm steeled his nerve. Sigurd may be the greatest of men, but all men are equally defenceless in sleep.

Again, Guttorm entered Sigurd's bed-chamber, only to flee a second time.

The mix of snake and wolf's meat in his stomach fueled his insanity, and at last, the boy found the courage to commit his horrendous task.

Moonlight shone through the open window onto the sleeping figure of Sigurd, who rested on his back.

Guttorm approached, brandishing the blade high.

Before he could think, he thrust the sword down through Sigurd's chest. The blade pierced clean through the man and into the mattress below.

Sigurd woke with a start and stared at Guttorm.

Guttorm gasped in horror at what he had done. He turned to flee.

Sigurd reached for Gram and threw it.

The legendary weapon, the sword that had killed Fafnir, sailed sideways through the air and cut Guttorm in half.

His legs separated from his torso, and the boy's entrails spilt all over the floor.

The clattering of the sword on the ground woke Gudrun.

She wailed when she saw her husband's impaled body. Scarlett blood flowed from him, turning the bed crimson.

Sigurd spoke to his wife as if he weren't breathing his last breaths. "Our son will grow to be the greatest ally they could have if they let him live. You must try to save him, for this wickedness surely falls upon Sigmund too. I regret to have been betrayed in such a manner by those I called brothers. Had I been able to stand and face my enemies, all of them would've died before me. I have never been unfaithful to you, and I have loved you as wholly as I could. Do not despair in my death."

He gently wiped a tear from the side of Gudrun's face. "This fate was long ago foretold, yet I refused to believe. Guide my son to be a greater man than I, for no one will be better to ride with. May the strength that I was blessed with in life now pass to him in death."

Gudrun sobbed. "Brynhild did this. She has loved you more than anyone has ever loved anything. There will be no greater man than you. Though you have not died this night in glorious battle, I hope Valhalla takes you," Gudrun cried.

Sigurd smiled, then rested his head back against the pillow. Darkness took him.

Earth's mightiest warrior was dead.

ᛋᛁᛈᚾᚱᛏᛘ ᚻᚾᚱᛁᚾᛪ

PART TWO

ᛁᚠ ᛏᚪᛶᛂ ᚦᛈᛏᛁᚱᚠᛁᛂ

CHAPTER 10

THE JOURNEY ONWARDS

The pain of the blade was gone.

Sigurd found himself standing in a misty courtyard of dark stone. It felt like he was waking from a perilously long sleep. Days, years, or lifetimes could've passed and he would not be aware. He did not recognise his surroundings yet knew where he was.

This was Helvegr, the Road to Hel. While in life, warriors spoke with a longing desire too battle forever in Valhalla, none spoke too openly about Hel. Sigurd had little idea what would face him on the journey down. Nor did he have any idea what awaited in the afterlife proper.

Sigurd looked down at his hands. His skin looked like it did in life. Veins pulsing with blood still crisscrossed his forearms. Despite appearing perfectly normal, he felt pale, like he was a mere shade of his former self.

He was empty.

Sigurd had hoped to die a glorious death in battle, as all noble men should. Despite his lifetime of heroism, here he now stood, in the cold embrace of the afterlife reserved for the ordinary. He wondered with deep regret how it had come to this.

It was difficult to see down the road blanketed in fog. In Sigurd's youth, Regin had once stated what the Road to Hel looked like, though in no certain terms. Sigurd knew it travelled through mist-laden valleys and fields void of light, but what came after was a mystery.

Sigurd sat on the ground and thought for a long moment. Thought of the life he'd left behind, his kingdom and treasures, and his wife and child consumed him. Already the cold air was dulling his senses. It was as if concern about mortal affairs was being pulled from his body.

Sigurd heard the sound of approaching footsteps and readied himself to face a monster, though he was weaponless.

The footsteps were small and light. He figured they most likely belonged to a woman. He ducked behind a large stone, not wanting to risk discovery in this place. The shame of being killed unaware drove his momentary cowardice, and Sigurd felt rightfully ashamed.

A woman had wandered into the same courtyard, oblivious to Sigurd's earlier presence.

Sigurd gasped when he saw it was Brynhild. She had followed him to the afterlife, probably hoping she could now claim his love. Sigurd didn't hate Brynhild for what she had set in motion; still, he had no desire to speak with her.

Sigurd waited for a long time before Brynhild left the

courtyard, disappearing into the mists along the road. He decided he would wait further still so he could not accidentally catch up with the treacherous woman.

Hours stretched into days as Sigurd waited, contemplating the success of his life and the failure of his death.

When at last all thoughts of home and love had faded from his mind, Sigurd began his search to find the halls of Hel.

For nine long days, he travelled without the need for food or sleep. He fumbled blindly in the dark, scrambling over boulders and navigating treacherous ravines by feeling alone.

On his tenth day, a bright light ignited the gloom. Its source remained a mystery as nothing penetrated the perpetually black sky above. Sigurd moved through a wasteland, which eventually turned into fertile fields abundant with herbs and vines. Further, he travelled, crossing a wide torrent that flowed with the weapons of warriors bouncing in its rushing waves.

He knew this bridge. It was called Gjallarbru and it crossed the River Gnoll. The legends Regin had told Sigurd as a boy stated that this was the point of no return. Sigurd knew this was the fate of all those who travelled to Hel. There was no reason to turn back now.

Once he'd crossed the bridge, Sigurd came to a battlefield where hundreds of souls fought. In a moment of sheer elation, he thought he was in Valhalla, but it wasn't so. This was a place of misery, where the lifeless dead repeated the same actions over and over. Sigurd approached the soul of an elderly warrior and asked him what this place was, but the man did not reply.

Sigurd moved on and the cold mists returned in such

density the land was smothered. Only the road remained free of obstruction. That was at least until he met the giantess.

Like Skrymir, Lord of Utgard, this giant was around fourteen feet tall. She wore a dress pieced together from different animal hides and carried a fearsome expression. She had a rough, unorthodox beauty, though the huge iron club she gripped tightly distracted from her feminine features.

Sigurd stopped before her. She stood as a formidable guard between the towering walls of mist.

"I am Modgudr. I guard the way forward. The living do not pass this point."

"I am Sigurd, slayer of Fafnir. Were it not for the blade that pierced my chest, I would still count myself among the living."

"Word of your death precedes you. Hel requests an audience. Follow the road."

Modgudr stepped aside, vanishing into the fog and Sigurd strode forward. Every hundred metres he travelled, the mist lessened.

Soon, Sigurd could see a towering wall of crimson stone looming high above him. Further in the distance, were the tall, dark spires of a formidable castle.

The wall was gargantuan and fashioned so it looked to have enormous black talons fixed to its ramparts that pointed menacingly downwards.

At last, Sigurd came to a gate wrought with black iron. It was tall enough to allow giants to pass comfortably. Another figure now blocked the road.

It was a rather large dog, one Sigurd knew to be named

Garmr. Garmr looked like a mix of a wolf and a domesticated breed, though abnormal in size. Garmr was the personal companion of the Goddess Hel, but today it seemed he was guarding the gate.

Sigurd looked at the dog and spoke, "Will you let me pass, beast?"

Garmr growled, bearing his teeth. He spread his four legs wide as if bracing for an attack.

"I will not wrestle you today," Sigurd smiled. He reached out confidently and stroked Garmr's head. The dog relaxed, whimpered, and moved out of the opening.

When Sigurd ran his fingers through the dog's soft fur, he felt a strange twinge of destiny.

Sigurd passed through the gate into Hel proper. At last, he was in the place his spirit would linger until it eventually faded away, or so he thought.

CHAPTER II

BALDR AND HEL

Hel had a deep blue sky ringed with stars. Sigurd assumed this to be a magical illusion, as he knew he was deep in the bowels of the Earth. Bright light from an unknown source filtered down, illuminating fields, villages and small cities rolling into the infinite distance. The bleating of goats and the clucks of chickens carried on the soft breeze. There were abundant farms. People wearing winter furs and patterned armour casually walked to and fro, attending to life-like chores.

It was not at all what Sigurd had expected.

A tall pointed castle like Sigurd had never seen was in the centre of it all. It looked to have been constructed with impossibly high, thin rectangular blocks. Each turret was topped with strange gnarled spires that reached up into the blue canvas above.

"An odd home for an odd deity," Sigurd thought.

He, of course, knew the story of Hel from his childhood.

Hel and her two brothers were beings of such power the gods had separated them in the world's far corners. Hel was the God of Death and had dominion over the Underworld. According to the old tales, she was the least monstrous of the three children of Loki.

One of her brothers was a mighty black wolf destined to eat the sun and moon. He was Fenrir the destroyer, who had long ago been bound in unbreakable bonds and buried somewhere deep in Asgard.

The other was Jormungandr, the World Serpent. He swam the oceans of Midgard, so large and terrifying that he wrapped around the world.

Sigurd was removed from his train of thought by a sudden rush of wind and a slight popping sound.

A man cloaked in brilliant yellow light had appeared ten feet ahead of him. With a long golden beard and swathes of curly hair, the man could only be one thing; a god. And a very recognisable god at that. His sculpted face and serene beauty were the telltale signs that this was the dead God of Light, Purity and Joy. This was Baldr.

"Welcome to Hel, Sigurd – greatest of men," Baldr beamed.

"Baldr," Sigurd mumbled, somewhat astonished to be greeted by such a renowned figure. "I am honoured."

"The honour is mine to meet such a fabled hero. Your legend will only grow from this point on."

Baldr, in his life, was known as the most beautiful of the gods. He'd been loved by all. Yet he was tormented by dreams of his own death.

Worried for her son, the Goddess Frigg went to every

object in Midgard, both living and non-living, and had them swear oaths they would never harm him. Either by mistake or arrogance, Frigg neglected the simple vine, mistletoe. When Loki learned of this, he constructed a spear of mistletoe and saved it for the right occasion.

The time came that the Aesir threw a feast. Much drinking and merriment were had, and in the joy of it, the gods started throwing things at Baldr to test his invulnerability. Arrows, swords and even Thor's hammer bounced off him.

Loki approached the blind deity Hodd, who was upset that he couldn't partake in the fun. In the guise of pity, Loki placed the spear in Hodd's hand and directed him in the direction of Baldr.

After a mighty throw, Baldr lay dead on the floor and so the world wept for him. Despite attempts to return Baldr to life, he could never leave Hel.

"Hel does not look as miserable as foretold," Sigurd said.

Baldr nodded. "This is not a place of punishment. There are paths from here that lead to Niflheim, where the evil dead dwell. Down there are terrors which we are far removed from. This is a place of peace."

"What do I do now that I am dead?" Sigurd asked. He'd been pondering this quite a lot on his journey here.

"Whatever you please. First, you must meet Hel. Follow me to the castle; we call it the House of Hel," Baldr said.

Sigurd was swept from his feet as if carried by a magical invisible wind. He flew across the land towards the carved wooden doors of the House of Hel.

He was deposited inside the entry chamber and was stunned

by the perplexing duality of the castle. It was as if he were standing on the divide of two entirely separate buildings. The right wall was blindingly white with silver arches and blazing torches. The left wall was black, with tattered bricks and the look of neglect and decay. It took a moment for Sigurd to attune himself to the bizarre layout.

Baldr led Sigurd up winding stairs and through great halls of mismatched stone. There wasn't another soul like him to be seen. In the dark corners and deep shadows of the architecture lurked horrible creatures. Draugr, undead bodies, aimlessly wandered the halls as they shuffled and groaned. Some held weapons and wore horned helmets. Others had glorious shields fixed to their arms which clanged against ancient breastplates. All were decayed and rotten, emitting vile smells.

Sigurd passed close to one and observed its rotten yellow teeth and stretched brown skin. Its eyes glowed a hypnotic blue.

"You said this was a place of peace," Sigurd began, "yet there is no peace in these undead monsters."

"These draugr were bewitched in Midgard. When a hero wrestles one back into its grave, they come here. Do not draw too close, for they possess many unnatural abilities and formidable magic," Baldr warned.

Sigurd gave the undead horde a wide berth from then on.

At last, they came to a circular room of one design. There was no duality here. Though made of grey stone, the room didn't look like a room. It was like Sigurd and Baldr were standing inside a tree, with long roots running up and down the walls.

In the centre of everything was a pit of blue flame. Strange foreign images fluttered into existence in the dancing fire.

"Sigurd of the Volsung line, meet Hel, Goddess of Death."

A figure cloaked in shadow stepped out from behind the immense well of flame. She was petite and feminine, wearing a simple billowing dress.

Despite being prepared for Hel's appearance, Sigurd was still taken aback.

Hel encompassed the duality of the castle. Split vertically down the middle of her body, her right half was that of a beautiful woman with silky black hair. Her left half was a decayed corpse, with a vacant white eyeball and necrotic black skin stretched over exposed fragments of bone.

Sigurd bowed low.

Hel had a gloomy, downcast expression. "Lord Sigurd, not often is it that a man of your legacy comes utmost downward and northward to my lands."

"Betrayal and treachery led to my death," Sigurd stated, trying to avoid looking at Hel's face.

"A man who sent many to Valhalla is denied it himself… funny how these things work out," Hel said, reaching out and running her dead fingers through the blue flames.

"During the journey here, I felt the weight of purpose and loss leave me…"

"In the afterlife, you no longer require such burdens. Even Baldr, who is a god and resistant to the magic of these lands, soon came to accept his place."

Baldr nodded.

Sigurd noticed a sad sweetness in Hel's voice; she did not sound demonic or evil.

"Odin placed me here when I was a young girl. Through his will alone, I became the Goddess of Death because he feared my appearance. I have no desire to inflict misery in death on those who lived decent lives."

"What becomes of us here?" Sigurd asked.

"In time, all things fade. Spirits linger longer if their impact in life was greater. You will be here for a long time, Sigurd," Hel stated.

Sigurd felt a small swell of pride at these words. Was his legacy really going to be remembered for so long in history?

"What do I do with myself now?" Sigurd asked.

"There are no wars to wage or lands to conquer for you anymore. Think of the lesser dreams you had in life and enact them. You can still eat, drink, and sleep in these lands, though you will never feel crippling hunger or exhaustion beyond measure."

Sigurd smiled. While he was denied an existence of glorious battle in Valhalla, an eternity in Hel was beginning to sound relaxing.

"My son and my wife…" Sigurd began, but Hel cut him off.

"Children go to another place. Your child fell victim to the same devious plot you did and has passed from life. In time, Gudrun will come to this place too."

Sigurd felt a torrent of anger rise in his stomach for the first time since he'd been dead.

"Do not pity the dead; they have no need for it," Baldr said, reassuringly.

Even with the magic in the air, Sigurd's sadness for the death of his son did not vanish quickly.

"Permit me to climb the rocky walls of Hel back to Midgard

so that I may take vengeance on those who wronged me," Sigurd said.

"Were it that I could grant such a request," Hel smiled sadly.

"I searched for a long time for a way to escape this place," Baldr said, looking sullen. The light that coated him dimmed slightly. "There are many paths in the deep places of Hel, though none can take you where you seek."

"But, you are a warrior. I know in life you held a mighty blade, Gram. That sword now belongs to the mortal who claims it next, but I can give you new weapons in death," Hel said.

She reached both her arms forward. Like a shimmering mist, clouds of silver and black sprung into being around her. The gasses combined in a shower of sparks and began to solidify. In her hands formed two silver axes patterned with red on the blades. Golden lines ran down the long handles, reminding Sigurd of his weapons and armour in life.

"These are Hel-wrought axes," Hel stated.

She walked forward and thrust them into Sigurd's hands.

She then waved her right hand and a simple sling appeared. It was leather and designed to be worn across the back to hold the axes. The sling magically wrapped itself across Sigurd's torso.

Sigurd marvelled at his new treasures.

"Consider these a gift for a noble life well lived. May they serve you in death as Gram did in life."

"Words cannot express my gratitude," Sigurd stated. He deposited the axes into his new sling and bowed low.

"Go and enjoy your death," Hel said. "If a day comes that I should need a champion, I will call upon you."

Hel and Baldr bade Sigurd farewell. The goddess offered Sigurd a room in the castle and an invitation to her frequent feasts for the dead.

Sigurd navigated his way down the sharp bends of the castle and before long stood on the infinite ever-green field. He was at last at peace.

CHAPTER 12

THE HEL'S HORNS

Years passed as Sigurd wandered the lands of Hel.

In time, his mind drifted back to his first conquest. He remembered sitting in the mead hall with his generals and his fleeting desire to live a simple life. The owner of that longhouse had satiated their thirst with fine mead and a joyous night had been had. That barman had a purpose alien to anything Sigurd had ever known.

Resigned to an idea, Sigurd embarked on a carefully considered project. Time and status had always prevented him from achieving it, but here neither of those things were his concern anymore.

He felled tall trees with his new Hel-wrought axes and stripped the bark from them. Sigurd placed the logs in an empty field and considered the layout of his new structure.

He was going to build a tavern.

Sigurd already had the name: The Hel's Horns.

Now that he wasn't a king who had to wage wars and fight enemies, he could finally indulge in this bold idea. Several magical flowers and grains grew in Hel and Sigurd was sure he could learn to use them to brew mead and beer. Some of the other souls down here would be valuable in that regard.

The days were long and Sigurd's muscles ached. He frequently worked till a mortal man would've collapsed from exhaustion. It was odd to be dead and still be somewhat tired.

Baldr explained that Hel had been modelled as a replica of life in Midgard. Other realms of the dead didn't take this approach, for apparently there were many underworlds.

Baldr said they were all connected with one main underworld, run by a group known as the Greek pantheon. Regions like Hel were wholly locked off from the Greek underworld, though if one knew the secret paths, they could travel out of Hel. Baldr admitted that it would be impossible to move between the realms without the power of a living god.

While Sigurd found the metaphysical structure of death interesting enough, his primary focus was completing the Hel's Horns. Further years drifted by as he learned to sculpt wood into detailed images and mastered carpentry. He learned to brew drinks celebrated throughout Hel.

In death, Sigurd became a different man. He frequently encountered faces from his life who reminded him of the man he used to be. He was glad to no longer be a king.

Regin appeared one day and aided him in creating metal furnishings for the Hel's Horns.

The dwarf repeated the sentiment that Sigurd had always known. In death, the grudges and debts of life no longer mattered. He admitted to planning to murder Sigurd moments before his head was lopped off.

Regin stated that Fafnir was in Niflheim, where vengeance and negativity festered like a plague. He warned Sigurd not to travel to those frozen depths at any cost. Though treacherous in life, the dwarf's words were now sincere.

Sigurd never encountered Brynhild. He figured her Valkyrie origins meant she must've gone somewhere other than Hel. He did feel a pang of regret at this, as they'd never cleared the air between them.

There came a day that a beautiful woman appeared in Sigurd's work area. Gudrun had at last passed from the lands of the living and arrived in Hel. The two embraced warmly, and they spoke at length about Gudrun's miserable life after Sigurd's death. The magic in the air meant they were not sour about such things for too long.

With Gudrun's help, Sigurd completed the Hel's Horns. It was a fine mead hall with a long centre table, a roaring fire and a thatched roof.

Gudrun helped Sigurd assemble large barrels to brew beer and mead.

The tavern became a popular place for the dead to gather. Souls came and spoke in length about their lives to Sigurd. Sometimes, they never came back, for it had come time for them to fade away.

Sigurd even met his descendants, (thanks to his surviving

daughter Aslaug) some of which were warriors with equal acclaim as him. Around this time, people started calling Sigurd a Viking, a term he'd never been called in life.

He was frequently invited to the House of Hel to discuss matters of importance with the gods. He and Baldr sometimes fought in the spirit of competition, though Sigurd was always outmatched by the god. During this time, Sigurd's fighting abilities became even more honed. He learned that a warrior must react instinctually when facing a divine foe. Their ability to shape the world around them meant thinking was a disadvantage.

Dead giants, dwarves and elves sometimes called on Sigurd to deal with clans of demons causing problems or draugr who'd appeared from Midgard.

Sigurd counted himself blessed that Gudrun's memory was tied to his own legend, so she would be around as long as he was. He took great comfort in this. In death, he lived the simple life he never could've while he walked the Earth. He was content for this to stay this way forever.

Then came a day that everything changed; the day the Underworld was attacked.

CHAPTER 13

HEL REMADE

A colossal shaking woke Sigurd from his slumber. This night he wasn't sleeping in the back of the Hel's Horns, as he so often did, but in the House of Hel after a spirited evening of competition with other noble spirits.

He'd always had restful nights in Hel's castle, so was surprised to feel his room trembling.

Though, it didn't feel like it was just his room.

The entire structure seemed to be heaving back and forth on its foundations.

Sigurd quickly dressed, equipping his two silver axes to the sling on his back. He rushed in the direction of Hel's council room.

He met Baldr in the entry hall, making the same fraught journey.

"What is happening to the castle?" Sigurd asked the dead

god.

"It isn't just the castle; the entire Underworld is shaking. Hel will be able to see."

They pushed through the doors into Hel's council chamber, where a small congregation had gathered around the roaring blue fire.

Unfamiliar visions flashed in the flames, which the goddess studied intently.

"Lady Hel, what news?" Baldr asked.

"War," Hel answered simply, stroking the large dog Garmr on the head. "Baldr, see to it that the spirits of the dead are armed and prepared for combat. Hades has fallen to a foreign force. As we speak, they are reassembling their legions to spread into the other lands of the Underworld. They will be here soon."

"What is that?" Sigurd asked aghast, pointing at the monstrous creature in the blue flames.

"A weapon of absolute destruction."

Sigurd watched as a gigantic seven-headed dragon swooped over green fields and forests, turning them all to ash in its torrents of fire. It was so perplexingly enormous it made Fafnir look like an earthworm.

"The Greeks have fallen? How?" Baldr asked.

"The angels of Heaven have increased their strength enough to challenge gods. The cosmic balance has shifted."

"Are there archangels? How many are we dealing with?"

"Just one," Hel replied. "The mightiest of their order, Michael, leads this host. His brother, Lucifer, was swallowed by a primordial deity. He is trapped in fire and darkness now."

Sigurd was overwhelmed with names he didn't recognise. Heaven? Michael?

"I don't understand," Sigurd said. "If we are under attack, where are the Aesir? Bring Odin and Thor to this battle!"

Hel's dead blank eye gazed at him, and she answered, "Within the mortal world exists a powerful empire based in the city of Rome. The emperor, on his deathbed, has converted to a rebellious new religion. This action has given them the power to declare war on the old order. I fear that if one archangel is here, more must be in Asgard."

"Good," Baldr stated. "If they are fighting this war on multiple fronts, then we have a chance to defeat them."

"But what do they have to gain from attacking the dead? We all eventually fade away anyway."

"It isn't about the souls here, Sigurd. The forces of Heaven have long sought to bend the world to their will. It starts by conquering the Underworld, where all the dead go, and reshaping it to their design. Control death, and through fear, you control life."

"How can that be? Those who linger long enough down here are meant to wait for Ragnarok, aren't they? That is the ultimate end to everything."

"History is changing," Hel stated simply.

The goddess turned to her dog, Garmr, who whimpered as he looked up at her.

"Garmr, go to the secret door in Niflheim and await the arrival of the gods from Midgard and Asgard. When they hear of this, they will come. Guide them here."

Garmr barked affirmatively, then sprinted away.

"Should we be overwhelmed, we will fall back to that door," Baldr said. With a pop, he vanished to fulfil Hel's original request of him.

"What would you have me do?" Sigurd asked Hel.

"I would have you fight. When the angels breach Hel, cut them from the sky."

"What are angels?"

"Winged men in golden armour. The spirits of the dead have given them some trouble already."

Sigurd felt for his axes. His heart had longed for a proper battle again, and now it was here.

Sigurd left the House of Hel.

First, he needed to find Gudrun. He would take her to Hel's castle, where she would be safe. An eternity without her was a thought Sigurd wasn't willing to entertain anymore.

A bright light filled the sky as hundreds of portals ripped open. Electricity sparked around their borders, creating an odd lightning storm high above. Winged men began funnelling through them.

They spread their magnificent wings wide, each glowing with blinding light. Their golden helmets and breastplates were exquisitely made and shimmered. Chariots pulled by winged horses blasted over the green fields as souls awoke to the sounds of this new terror.

The dead were caught by surprise as torrents of arrows, made entirely of light, rained down from above.

Emitting his own brilliant light, Baldr took to the air and began performing a complex spell.

The empty fields and open plains between the crimson outer water of Hel's domain and her castle brimmed with the souls of the dead. From all across the afterlife, they'd been summoned to fight. Giants roared and elves drew their bows. Since it wasn't only humans here, there was powerful magic on both sides.

The gate in the wall came crashing down as the giantess, Modgurdr, burst through it, waving her iron club high.

The battle had begun.

In the chaos of it all, Sigurd managed to pick up a bow and quiver and slung them around himself. He drew his axes and ran for the nearest giant.

"Throw me up!" he ordered.

The giant gripped Sigurd, then tossed him into the air.

He sailed into the cloud of angels, digging his axes into one. They floated downwards, with Sigurd using its broad wings like a parachute.

The people in Hel may not have died warrior's deaths, but that didn't mean they couldn't fight.

A storm of boulders thrown by giants forced the legions of angels close to the ground, where they had to engage in combat with the dead. Dwarven magic then locked them there, burning their wings away.

Many were like Sigurd, who hadn't died in battle but were skilled enough to have gone to Valhalla. Flurries of swords and axes caught the angels by surprise as the vicious souls tore them apart.

Sigurd leapt, cut and slashed his way through the angels with ease, dodging arrows and javelins made of light.

He laughed in the thrill of it all.

Through the chaos, he recognised Gudrun by her long chestnut hair. She'd also picked up a bow and quiver, though she looked very unsteady with it. She was with a group of armoured archers.

"Baldr," Sigurd shouted, drawing his own bow. "Raise us up!"

Baldr nodded, then rolled his arms upwards.

The ground heaved and groaned, then a tall column of earth erupted skywards at their feet.

Sigurd ordered the arches to blacken the sky with arrows.

Baldr's magic caught the attention of an angel that was different from the others. He had six white wings and looked thoroughly battle-worn. He wore a helmet in the shape of a roaring lion, and from his back flew the tattered remains of a shining cape.

The archangel rushed towards Baldr, who met him in mid-air. Baldr summoned an axe and struck at his foe, causing lightning to shoot across the battlefield.

"That must be Michael," Sigurd thought as he watched the divine figures brawl. They were almost of even skill, though Baldr had the upper hand.

Baldr's axe cut into Michael's lion helmet, splintering a chunk of it clean off. Michael kicked Baldr hard in the chest, then removed his helmet and tossed it into the chaos below.

Sigurd could see determination etched on the archangel's face. He could also see other emotions there, particularly nervous anxiety. It was almost as if the archangel was fearful, but not about Baldr... He wanted this battle over quickly for some unknown reason.

They tumbled close enough for Sigurd to hear them speak.

"Surrender," Michael spat. "You are not the first underworld we have conquered down here and you will not be the last."

"It is not our way," Baldr said. "Even in death, we have honour if we fade through battle."

"You were killed by your own kind!" Michael said incredulously. "They left you to linger as a shade of your former godly self! Join us, and I will see you restored to life and godhood. Many gods of the old order are on our side!"

"I am destined to lead the new world after Ragnarok. My end is not here," Baldr said simply.

"That is a fool's statement," Michael replied. "Ragnarok will never happen. Your time is at an end."

Baldr's serene face didn't betray his internal thoughts. Sigurd took a javelin from one of the men beside him and sent it hurtling at Michael.

When Michael moved to deflect it, Baldr struck again, turning and slamming his axe into Michael's chest.

The archangel's armour cracked. Baldr pulled his weapon free and swung it at Michael's head. This was to be the killing blow.

Michael bent backwards, narrowly avoiding the deadly attack. He aimed his sword at Baldr's chest, though he was momentarily stunned to see his blade simply bounce off the god.

"There is no weapon that can harm me," Baldr smirked.

"I did hear that was the case, so I came prepared," Michael smirked. He struck again, and Baldr parried the blow. They held their weapons against each other, pushing with equal might.

Michael then dropped his sword, and Baldr jolted forward

uncontrollably.

With his right hand, Michael drew a green dagger from his belt.

At once, Sigurd knew what it was. It was a blade made of mistletoe.

He looked on in horror as the archangel pressed it into Baldr's stomach. The god's eyes went wide with shock.

He then exploded in a pulse of dazzling amethyst energy that knocked every angel from the sky and every dead fighter to the ground.

Michael was knocked into the House of Hel at tremendous speed.

"No," Sigurd said quietly. Baldr was meant to live until Ragnarok and even beyond in the old stories. Destiny itself was being rewritten here.

Sigurd had been foolish. It was only now that he realised how unsafe they were.

There was no way down from the cliff Baldr had created.

Sigurd and his comrades again began firing arrows in all directions. Gudrun threw Sigurd a length of rope, and he dropped his bow.

He formed a noose and swung the lasso in the air, catching an angel around his ankles and pulling him down towards them.

"Angel," Sigurd yelled, "you will fly my wife off this cliff!"

Gudrun looked at him, amazed.

Then, another explosion rang out.

The House of Hel teetered on its foundations and began crumbling apart. Huge stones crashed into the earth in a series of resounding booms. A swarm of draugr emerged from the rubble to attack as a ravenous horde. They were on no one's side in this fight.

"Hel must have fallen!" Gudrun yelled.

Sigurd gulped. He'd never been on the losing side of a battle before. He wasn't sure how it had happened, but the battle had swiftly turned against them. The giants were running for cover as the airborne charioteers harassed them.

From high on the cliff, Sigurd watched as the angels overwhelmed the defenders of Hel. Cries of fear, pain and terror echoed across the land.

Then something odd happened. The angels began fleeing.

Sigurd heard their frantic yells of retreat.

"We took too long! We've drawn its attention!"

"Escape this realm now before it gets here!"

The surviving spirits looked confused. What were the angels talking about?

Michael burst from the crumpled ruins of the House of Hel at supersonic speed and began shouting also.

Sigurd could just make out the words.

"Distract it…. send it else-"

There was a colossal booming roar as the sky warped and stretched.

Everyone froze in place.

Like the tearing of fabric, a hole as wide as the curve of the sky was ripped open.

Enormous beyond comprehension, with scarlet scales and seven monstrous waving heads, a dragon entered Hel.

At once, each head sent forth a tornado of fire. The world

became fire. All of Hel withered in the beating of the impossible beast's wings.

Sigurd had seen this dragon in the blue flames at the start of the battle. It was an uncontrollable engine of destruction.

The dragon shrieked and the angels scarpered in a blind panic. A couple of its heads snapped at each other in annoyance.

The heat was quickly becoming unbearable as wildfires swallowed the lands of the dead.

The battling giants and skirmishing warriors below were incinerated. He saw the fire pass over the Hel's Horns, and it was blown apart.

Behind him, the archers on the cliff were set upon by a group of angels now fleeing the main arena of battle.

Sigurd turned in horror to see a shower of light arrows fall across them, several piercing Gudrun.

"NO!" Sigurd yelled.

Gudrun smiled at him. It was a strange smile, filled with an inexplicable mix of love and sadness. Then Gudrun faded into nothingness.

The warriors with him were cut down, all except Sigurd, who fought with such ferocity the angels began to retreat from him.

"Do not flee you, cowards!" Sigurd commanded, throwing his lasso around another angel.

He caught the winged man right as he opened a portal out of Hel, back to wherever he came from. Sigurd could see why. One of the monstrous dragon's heads looked right at them, jaws wide. An inferno was brewing in its mouth.

The angel dived into the portal, dragging Sigurd by his

length of rope through just before the wall of fire hit.

Sigurd's body twisted and warped as he zoomed from Hel into the greater underworld. It was like he was being pulled through a tube too tight for his body.

He emerged coughing and spluttering on the hard ground of a scorched wasteland. At once, he yanked on the rope and pulled the angel from the air, hacking it to pieces with his silver axes.

Then he sat alone and watched as angels streamed above him, oblivious to the single man's presence.

There was nothing in this new place. Just heat, desolation and emptiness. Sigurd's afterlife had just been stolen from him in a war that was beyond comprehension. What was he to do now?

CHAPTER 14

THE HELL KEY

Sigurd's escape to the wasteland left him feeling like a coward and traitor.

Everyone was gone. Gudrun's spirit had been obliterated. Their existence together had ended far quicker than it should have, and Sigurd felt cheated by this. Gudrun's name was tied to his, and while his legend endured, her spirit would've too.

The wasteland he'd come to sat on the far border of the wider Underworld, to which all other places of death (like Hel) were connected.

The angels assault had left it as a ruined burning stretch of nothingness.

Sigurd found sanctuary in the caves the ran deep into the grey cliffs around the wasteland. It was from these caves he felt the land crack, bend and shift. The entire Underworld trembled as the angels began a process of reformation. The great rivers were moved and diverted.

The high walls of the enormous cavern soon disappeared as the angel's created an artificial red sky above.

Years, in numbers beyond counting, passed for Sigurd in that place.

Stories from other survivors in the waste completed Sigurd's picture of what had happened in Hel. He learned that the angels had attacked every underworld, ripping open the dividing barriers and merging them all into one.

They were building a new realm where all the dead from across the world would go. It was, ironically, to be called Hell.

The angels enslaved demons from every culture, uniting them to shape the landscape.

The other wanderers, seldom encountered, didn't linger for long, with some fading from existence when their time had come. It was lonely for Sigurd, who'd always been surrounded by admirers and supporters.

Though Sigurd had no way to tell the passing of time, it felt like hundreds of years sailed by as he watched reality shift. The edge of the wasteland was marked by sheer cliffs that dived hundreds of feet onto an expansive plateau below.

It was on the plateau that the greatest of the construction works took place, though monsters proved a ever-present problem.

A few angelic soldiers remained around the wastes to keep the wild demon population in check.

Sigurd had frequent run-ins with the pale eyeless creatures. The wild demons scurried about the red rocks and seemed to huddle near the ruins of a destroyed city. If he didn't have his Hel-wrought axes, he would've had difficulty killing them when they attacked. The creatures seemed to have the barest hint of intelligence and were more like animals than anything else.

The angels had struggled to control them, so instead herded them into Sigurd's wasteland, away from the massive construction projects underway.

A day came when horns blew and a host of magnificent six-winged angels appeared, headed by Archangel Michael.

Sigurd took a perch on the high cliffs to see what was transpiring below. A tornado of black burst from a flat plain beneath his mountainous sanctuary. A wild wind whipped up and the air buzzed with electricity.

The wind died in a blast of black lightning, then there was a monumental crack as the ground splintered. Sigurd saw several small figures appear on the plateau below.

The archangels flew down to greet the newly emerged beings. Through whispers and legends, Sigurd was well aware of who these beings were.

Lucifer, the lost archangel, had returned.

Lucifer, and his team of angelic warriors, the Gladius Vaticanus, had been the prisoners of the primordial entity Tartarus.

Though Sigurd was too high to see in great detail, it was clear that none of them looked like angels anymore. They all seemed warped and disfigured. Hundreds of years of fire and darkness had twisted them into grotesque new shapes.

Other than an increase in the speed of the vast works below, the return of Lucifer had little impact on Sigurd's grim existence.

Sometimes, packs of angels and other kinds of demons

came to the wasteland, searching for something Sigurd didn't know. Sigurd, wearing his hooded tattered travelling cloak, approached them, seeking information, as they weren't always hostile.

For the most part, the angels and demons ignored the wasteland in which Sigurd lived.

The plateau below marked the border for the the First Circle of Hell, as that area came to be known. Everything outside of the First Circle of Hell was regarded as worthless territory. An enormous wall that stretched across the horizon was built. In front of it was a smaller walled city with a substantial spiralling tower in its centre.

The Underworld was divided into 'circles'.

Each consecutive circle sat beneath the first, further underground. They didn't need walls, instead being enclosed by a huge cylindrical cavern. Rivers flowed progressively downwards until they reached the Ninth Circle of Hell, a frozen wasteland at the bottom. Each Circle encompassed various regions, called 'rings' within them and were geographically unique. They also punished different crimes.

The city outside the First Circle barrier wall, once it was complete, brimmed with commerce and trade. This was the true frontier town of Hell.

It was not a large place, and the demons came to know Sigurd well. It was a wild and lawless place.

Occasionally Sigurd found objects of value in the wreckage of the wasteland, and traded for lumber and other imports from the mortal world.

Sigurd gathered enough materials to build a simple wooden

home in the waste. Though it was not much, it reminded him of his early years in Hel. That brought great comfort to the lonely warrior.

Then came a time when unplaced souls like Sigurd became hunted. No longer did every soul come to the Underworld. It became a place for sinners only, here for eternal punishment. Each Circle of Hell punished different crimes to varying degrees of intensity.

Some thought Sigurd to be a soul who'd escaped his just punishment. None bothered to think that his memory on Earth was so strong that he was from the time before Hell.

Sigurd became a rat in the walls, scurrying to survive.

When he grew bolder, he journeyed into the First Circle of Hell to scavenge for resources beyond the border wall. Demons, he could manage in a fight, but angels and the Gladius Vaticanus were far too powerful.

There were also gods in Hell who'd joined the angel's side, whether by their own will or force.

Sigurd has had to contend with a complex series of rules in this new Underworld.

Movement in Hell was restricted entirely to physical travel, so magically appearing and disappearing was impossible. There was an exception to this rule, however. One god, named Thanatos, a God of Death from the Mediterranean region, was the only creature that could move through Hell by magical flight and teleportation.

Sigurd's investigations into how Thanatos bypassed these rules revealed that he possessed a unique artefact. It was a key forged from hellfire with the very essence of Tartarus bound to it. Small, simple and white, the key looked like any other key as it dangled around Thanatos' neck. He was the chief being who determined the placement of souls in Hell and thusly needed to move with ease across it. Every time Sigurd saw the black-cloaked god, he looked sour and resentful. The denizens of Hell called him 'the Grim Reaper', a nickname that stuck.

Sigurd had some difficulty with stealth in his travels, being a huge man. However, he found that none would look at him twice in the right set of demon's armour.

The First Circle of Hell, all things considered, wasn't unpleasant. There were stone cities lined with grotesque idols and farms on their outskirts, though not much grew in the scorched land.

Sigurd's wanderings through this land taught him that the archangels only cared about rewarding and punishing souls of particular note in the new world order. People who'd lived ordinary lives, unless in exceptional circumstances, didn't even travel to an afterlife anymore. Their souls lingered for a little while in a disconnected purgatory, then faded into energy.

Deeper and deeper into Hell he travelled. Through unintended foolishness, Sigurd was revealed in the Fourth Circle. It was here that he first met and escaped the fallen angel, Belial. Belial was a wicked, monstrous being in the service of Lucifer that took delight in punishing others.

He and Belial would have many further run-ins in the years that followed.

Sigurd decided he could no longer journey without a way to combat the fallen angels, whose power level greatly exceeded his.

His answer to this complex problem came one day in the

outer-city near his home in the waste.

Sigurd had noticed that sometimes living mortals arrived through a portal in the outer-city for meetings with important figures in Hell. Often, they were escorted into the First Circle of Hell, then from there, down to wherever they needed to go.

They were met and guided by an odd-looking creature named Adramelech. He was an old Sumerian god with the body of a man and the head of a horse. From his rear end sprung a magnificent plume of peacock's feathers.

Adramelech and Sigurd had spoken before. Sigurd had asked Adramelech if the god could return him to the mortal world in the early days of construction. Adramelech had flatly denied his request, stating there were too many complications and old laws he didn't want to break.

One day, while Sigurd walked through the outer-city, he noticed that around Adramelech's neck swung a curious object. It was the Hell Key, the very same that Thanatos used to move freely through Hell.

Sigurd had never seen it so accessible before, and his desire to have it was great.

"Lord Adramelech," Sigurd said formally, approaching the horse-headed man.

"Oh, Sigurd, is that you?" Adramelech said, eyeing him closely.

"How could you tell?"

"Your bright eyes shine through your face plate. You know Belial has put a bounty on your head?"

"I am sure Belial is more concerned with convincing mortals

to torture and murder each other up above than with me."

"They call themselves the Knights of Hell these days, Lucifer's fallen angels," Adramelech said absent-mindedly. "They run the show down here. Don't much like themself."

All of the Knights of Hell, once beautiful angels, were uniquely twisted creatures that enjoyed almost absolute authority over the Underworld.

"Yes, word has reached my ears that they enjoy sending demons up to the mortal world to spread chaos and evil. We slew monsters like them in the days I walked the Earth."

"It is a different world up there now, Sigurd. In many ways, things have gone backwards. The shadow of Heaven looms over humanity. Still, Belial and his ilk cannot bother me."

"Why not?"

"This key," Adramelech said, his horse eyes gleaming as he pulled it forward. "Many wonderful properties it has. Transport, freedom of movement, but most importantly, it levels the playing field. Any creature of Hell, as those angels now are, will be brought down to the wearer's level, no matter what abilities they possess."

"That is a truly valuable item," Sigurd stated. "How did you get it?"

Adramelech leaned in close and said, "Thanatos fled. It isn't common knowledge yet. He abandoned his post, but they caught him in the mortal world. Rumour has it that Lucifer is now thinking of permanently stationing some of his knights on Earth because of this. I approached Lucifer and requested the key. You know there are multiple paths in and out of Hell. The official channels are easy for me to manage. But if a mortal creates their own portal or falls into a trap, they arrive at a check-in point high in the sky. It can be difficult for me to get there. The larger winged demons don't like to be ridden, you see."

"I will speak plainly," Sigurd said. "I desire that key more than any other item. Will you make a deal?"

"Oh-hoh! You have nothing of value to offer me in exchange for this!" Adramelech laughed.

"I would show my greatest trinket, but I dare not do it here. For the ring draws attention to itself."

Adramelech looked intrigued. "I will humour you, Sigurd the Viking. We will go to the point highest in Hell to talk."

Adramelech pointed the Hell Key forward, and with a spinning, tearing, sucking sound, a portal opened up before them.

Hesitantly, Sigurd stepped through it, followed by the old Sumerian god.

This new place was unlike anywhere Sigurd had seen in Hell. He was on a floating red island in a sea of grey mist.

Other rotating chunks of stone slowly spun all around.

"Well, show me what you have," Adramelech ordered.

Sigurd plucked a small golden ring from his finger and held it up.

"If you are familiar with my life, you know I owned the greatest treasure there ever was."

"You are saying this is Andvaranaut?" Adramelech murmured.

Sigurd smiled. The ring was merely a trinket he'd found long ago in the wasteland. The true Andvaranaut was in the mortal world somewhere, probably in the tomb of Gudrun.

"Isn't it cursed?" Adramelech asked.

"Yes, though I imagine that wouldn't matter to a god like you."

"And it works? It has the power to create gold and multiply treasures?"

"You know how hard it is to get simple comforts in Hell. This ring would see you living in a luxury beyond even Lucifer."

Sigurd looked over the edge of the red island. "Is there a way down from here?"

"No," Adramelech said distractedly. He fingered the key around his neck, looking at the ring greedily.

Hastily, he pulled the Hell Key's chain over his head and passed it to Sigurd. Sigurd took it and tossed the ring to Adramelech. The throw went wide and the god had to go back a few paces to get it.

As soon as Adramelech's back was turned, Sigurd thrust the key forward, just as the horse-man had done, and stepped through the portal.

Adramelech immediately realised Sigurd's deception. He looked horrified as he saw Sigurd step through the breach in reality and vanish. All that was left was a swirl of dust.

Sigurd appeared back at his wooden home in the wastes. He grabbed his Hel axes and attached their sling to his back.

Sigurd looked down at the simple white key and smiled.

For so long, he'd been constrained, living on the fringes of this world. Now it was time to take Hell by the horns.

The legend of Sigurd, Hell-warrior, was about to be born.

CHAPTER 15

ADVENTURES IN THE FIRE

From that day onwards, Sigurd once again became a person of note.

With the Hell Key dangling around his neck, Sigurd earned a reputation of notoriety throughout the burned regions of Hell. No longer was he a famous king known for noble deeds, but an outlaw and a rebel. The only part of his old life that remained true was his status as a formidable warrior.

He became a perpetual thorn in the sides of the Knights of Hell. Some of the creatures called him 'the mad Viking', for the way he seemed to tempt fate when no other would dare cross them.

Sigurd never saw Adramelech again. Lucifer was so enraged that the Sumerian god had lost the Hell Key so foolishly that he forbade any winged creature from flying up there to retrieve him.

Sigurd did his best to avoid provoking the wrath of Lucifer directly. He stayed well clear of the Ninth Circle of Hell, where

Lucifer took the form of a three-headed giant and watched the world from his seat of power.

While the magic of the Hell Key worked well enough on the Knights of Hell, he was sure there would never be an even playing field between himself and the Prince of Darkness.

Of course, the Knights of Hell scoured every corner of their domain to find his hiding spot. In their arrogance, they never considered looking beyond the Circles of Hell. Sigurd's wooden home in the wasteland remained a peaceful secret – a safe haven he could retreat to when his daring grew too much.

Rumours of the mad Viking's power grew from whispers, becoming legend. Hell creatures swore they saw Sigurd battle evenly with Belial, Astaroth, Leviathan and other powerful monsters, always escaping by the skin of his teeth. Sometimes, the rumours said, Sigurd was able to take down impossible foes. Giant monsters that squirmed and writhed in the deepest pits fell before his furiously swung axes.

High above, in the mortal world, Sigurd became a national hero to certain groups of Europeans. He was a mythical figure that displayed ideals people wanted to emulate. He was hailed as a beacon of courage and skill. Some of the creatures folded into Lucifer's regime called him heroic, too.

One day, while journeying through the Second Circle of Hell, Sigurd decided to pay a purposed visit to his friend Minos. It was challenging to find beings of value to call friends in Hell, but Minos was an honourable man.

Minos was an ancient Greek king who used to judge the souls of the damned when they entered the old Underworld. He'd survived the angels take over and been placed in charge of the Second Circle.

This was a land ravaged by fierce winds. An eternal tempest buffeted the lustful, for here dwelled those whose sins fell into the domain of lust.

The only relief from the deadly tornados and world-shaking hurricanes were a series of black towers scattered about the land. These towers emitted a deathly pale light that coated the Second Circle in an eerie glow.

It was inside the largest tower where Minos sat. Once every so often, he'd swing open the gates so that the punished could beseech him for mercy. This was not required of him, but Minos was never an evil man. He fought the system as best he could from within.

"Sigurd, I am glad you have come," Minos said. He looked unusually troubled.

"You seem gripped in the hand of dread," Sigurd stated, seeing the worry etched on his face.

"Belial is here, in the southernmost tower. Do you know the succubi?"

Sigurd was well aware of the succubi.

A succubus was a stunningly attractive woman, usually wearing shamefully revealing clothing. They were demons with leathery wings that sprouted from their backs and small pointed horns in their hair. They often caused trouble for mortals and, for some, were the direct reason they ended up in the Second Circle of Hell.

"I know the demon women, yes," Sigurd said.

"There is one in my service here, named Caahra, who was sent by Belial to tempt a noble mortal and cause his downfall. She fell in love with the man, believe it or not. This isn't the first time a succubus has failed. Belial will see to it that she is obliterated and I would not have it so. Caahra is one of the few servants I have of value in this miserable place."

"I do enjoy my run-ins with Belial," Sigurd laughed. "I will see the monster freed. In return, I would ask something of you."

"I'm happy to oblige," Minos bowed.

"I seek lumber, though nowhere in Hell seems to have it. Find me what wood you can. There is a project I'm working on."

"There are trees in some places. Can you not fell them?"

"No, the trees in Hell mostly turn to ash when you cut them down."

"I will think on this. Take Caahra somewhere safe; where Belial's yellow eyes will not see her."

Sigurd pointed his Hell Key forward, and a portal ripped itself open in the empty space. He jumped through it.

He stood in an ominous black room with tall square windows. The thick stone walls did little to dull the sound of the gale outside. An altar, lined with glowing red runes, sat on a platform in the room's centre. Atop the altar was a beautiful woman, squirming against her bindings. Her dress was torn to rags and she bore the telltale signs of violent struggle on her face.

No one else was here.

Sigurd rushed forward and drew one of his axes. He cut her free with a mighty chop, the magical axe slicing through her chains like they were made of butter.

"Caahra?" Sigurd asked.

"Yes, you are the mad Viking!" she said, a look of shock on her face.

"Let us get out of here before –"

"YOU!" a high voice screamed.

Sigurd turned to see a familiar figure. Red all over, with a bald head and spiralling black horns, was the fallen angel Belial. He had goat's legs, great black bat wings and a vivid green serpent for a tail.

"Why must YOU always INTERFERE!" Belial roared. "Do you do it just to annoy me?"

"I do what I can to annoy you," Sigurd shrugged.

"Well, you have made a mistake this time. This room is lined with binding runes."

Belial waved his hand and Sigurd was bathed in red light. The whole place ignited in the glow of previously hidden magical symbols.

"I doubt even your stolen key will allow you to leave now."

Belial raised his right arm and a sword of fire manifested in his hand.

Sigurd released the succubus and gripped his other axe.

"This time, I will kill you," Belial sneered.

Belial shot towards Sigurd at supersonic speed, knocking him off his feet. He tried to thrust his fiery sword into Sigurd's chest, but the Viking blocked it with his magical axes.

He rolled to the side then got to his feet, launching a kick into Belial's stomach.

They threw strikes at each other with vicious ferocity.

Thanks to the magic of the Hell Key, Belial was no stronger than Sigurd. They were evenly matched, though the angel did have supernatural powers.

Belial sucked in a breath and let out a scorching torrent of fire. The succubus, Caahra, jumped in Sigurd's way; her wings spread and absorbed the brunt of the attack. She flopped to the floor, gravely injured.

Sigurd leapt over her and brought his axe down on Belial. The blade sliced into the knight's skin, causing him to squeal in anguish.

Sigurd felt the air ripple with power.

Belial hunched over.

Sigurd had seen this before. The fallen angels could create a colossal explosion of energy that would undoubtedly destroy the dark tower.

Sigurd ran backwards and scooped up Caahra in his arms. He dived out of the nearest window, glass shards falling around him.

As soon as he was free of the room, he thrust the key forward and a portal opened before them. They fell vertically through it.

They crashed hard into the floor of Sigurd's wasteland home.

"Where are we?" Caahra asked, rubbing her head furiously.

"Somewhere safe," Sigurd replied. "I will see to your burns."

From that moment on, Sigurd and Caahra became firm friends.

It was odd to have a demonic monster for an ally. Sigurd

began to look at the world less black and white. Caahra actually made for pleasant company, being able to speak with all the eloquence and wisdom of a long-lived mortal. Though, when she took to the air to hunt the pale animalistic demons, Sigurd stayed far away. The sound of her crunching through bone and ripping off long flesh tears was nauseating.

Her wings made her a helpful ally, being able to scout from high above to find objects Sigurd desired. Minos came through with a large delivery of timber, which Sigurd found exceedingly useful.

• • • • •

A few decades later, while still working on the same project, Sigurd found himself in a similar situation. This time it wasn't Belial, instead the Knight of Hell Leviathan, who took the form of an enormous sea serpent.

When in Hell, Leviathan slithered through the dirty waters of the Fourth Circle, where the greedy were punished.

Because the swamps of the Fourth Circle contained a myriad of trees, Sigurd often went there in attempts to find ones that could be cut down for wood. It was a challenging task, though occasionally, he was successful. Sometimes a fallen tree didn't explode into grey dust, and he could use it.

While he journeyed through the swamps, he met the Japanese water demon named Kanto. Kanto was a kappa, a bipedal turtle-like creature with a shallow bowl on his head filled with water.

Sigurd spied the creature standing by a vast stretch of river through the dense trees.

He approached.

"Tell me, demon, what brings you here?"

The kappa looked at him with its round black eyes and said, "You should leave this place. I am waiting for punishment from the Knight of Hell Leviathan."

"What have you done to deserve punishment from that wretched creature?"

"Leviathan has been spending his time in the mortal world of late. He sinks ships off the Japanese coast. I warned a family of his presence, and he was denied victims. He called me into Hell to await his return."

"Leviathan will swallow you whole. You should leave here."

"I cannot. There is nowhere he will not find me."

The water rippled menacingly and an enormous blue head burst forth. His looming shadow darkened the trees. Leviathan was covered in blue scales with bright red fins. He had a long-hooked beak and jaw lined with gargantuan razor-sharp teeth.

His eyes darted from the kappa to Sigurd.

He released a deep thudding groan and plunged his head towards the Viking. Sigurd had to dive into the water to avoid the crushing bite.

What followed was an impossible battle between Sigurd and the sea serpent. Though equal in strength, Leviathan's size made him tough to handle.

Sigurd much prefered to tackle Leviathan when he was in his more human form. He looked more like a drowned corpse than anything else. Sigurd, feeling sure he couldn't win against the gargantuan serpent, took a different option for victory. He grabbed the kappa and teleported out of there.

The kappa proved to be honourable as well. Just like that, Sigurd now found himself living with two demons. He trusted them completely, against his better judgement.

• • • • •

Once Sigurd was sure he could trust Kanto and Caahra, he revealed his plan to them. In the Seventh Circle of Hell, he'd been secretly building a place of his own.

He was, in fact, recreating the Hel's Horns Tavern. Now called the Hell's Horns.

Sigurd had discovered the ruins of a city once called Sodom many centuries ago.

Sodom was the trading hub of Hell, and Sigurd had become a familiar figure in the crowds of imps and minotaurs that wandered the ruined streets. Apparently, the city had faced apocalyptic divine wrath, then been transported to Hell.

Much to Sigurd's pleasure, he learned all kinds of creatures conducted deals and sought shelter there. He'd met shadow demons, ghouls and oni, among endless other beings.

It was the perfect place for him to recreate his tavern. No longer was her possessed by the thoughts of living another life that pushed him to build it again. The memory of Gudrun lingered in Sigurd's mind. Rebuilding the Hell's Horns reminded him of when he was at peace in the afterlife, with her by his side.

His main problem was resources. He'd found enough wood for some of it, Minos having supplied a good deal. But there wasn't enough to complete the job.

The Knights of Hell were never seen in the city, for they found the affairs of demons beneath them.

The ever-growing population of punished souls took their attention. Some of the fallen angels enjoyed using them for their own purposes, with the Knight of Hell Astaroth forming a veritable army of construction workers with the punished dead, not far from Sodom.

The pressure from the Knights of Hell grew even less in the year 1300 when five of them departed permanently for the mortal world, Belial and Leviathan among them.

Hell was being sealed off permanently, with magical barriers being put in place so that only dead mortals could come in and none could leave. This caused a furore among imps and other malevolent spirits who frequently moved between the plains of existence.

The downside of this was that attention was drawn to the Hell's Horns. By the year 1300, the tavern was long finished and became iconic.

Caahra and Kanto had sourced unconventional building materials, which Sigurd heartily disliked.

For example, one of his walls was made of a pulsating fleshy substance that seemed alive. He had built traditional long benches like he'd seen in life. He'd also been gifted enchanted black tables with high stools that gave off a sinister aura.

Sigurd brewed the drinks himself, teaching Caahra and Kanto his secret recipes. He had the daring to dig a hole down to Lucifer's frozen wasteland, so they could collect ice.

The Hell's Horns wasn't a Viking mead hall in appearance,

but it was so in spirit. Hell creatures came to drink and fight, with Sigurd often besting the best of them.

The scrapers, traders and wanderers of Hell saw Sigurd as a useful tool to acquire resources once the mortal world was shut off. The benefits of these transactions flowed both ways.

While Sigurd had no innate fondness for demons or the other creatures that dwelled in the fire, he did form alliances with the lesser of the evil beings. Sigurd was well-respected, even becoming a leader of the odd assembly of creatures that used Sodom as a refuge.

Sigurd's influence grew to the point that at last Lucifer, who'd been oblivious for so long, took interest.

• • • • •

Sigurd woke one morning in his wooden home and wearily dressed. Once equipped with his trademark axes, he thrust the key forward and opened a portal to the Hell's Horns.

He wearily greeted Caahra, not noticing the petrified look on her face. Kanto, too, seemed oddly quiet.

"What has upset you two?" Sigurd asked.

Kanto pointed his slimy arm forward, and Sigurd was shocked to see a handsome man sitting on one of his high stools.

He was a figure of pristine beauty, though his eyes were blood red. He also sported six great red wings jutting from his back. He wore a simple black robe trimmed with gold and smiled pleasantly when Sigurd noticed him. The stranger's long hair framed each side of his face, and he casually brushed it aside to look upon the old king better.

"At last, we meet," Lucifer said, getting to his feet and approaching.

He was at least a foot shorter than Sigurd when he started walking, but they were eye to eye after a few steps.

"Lord Lucifer," Sigurd said, struggling to contain his inner sense of dread.

"Let us dispense with formality," Lucifer said politely. "Obviously, I have heard the gripes from my Knights of Hell about you. You are an annoying insect in need of swatting, though they have been unable to do it."

"My life was noble and my death has certainly been interesting. If now is my time to fade from the world, then I do so with no regrets."

"I have no desire to destroy you," Lucifer said, casually strolling around the cluttered room. "Your story in death is perhaps, as you say, more interesting than it was in life. And I sense greater purpose from you still, though I don't know what it is."

"Then why have you come?" Sigurd asked.

"As you know, five of my Knights of Hell now reside permanently in the mortal world. The remaining three in Hell are here to ensure things run as I wish. The world is turning quickly, and I, too, look beyond the borders of Hell for my future. For my plans to work, the Knights of Hell must be able to do their jobs without interference."

Sigurd suddenly felt like he would get off relatively lightly, considering all he'd done since Lucifer took over.

"You will not interfere with the business of Hell again. I

will not tell my servants about your pet project here in Sodom as a sign of goodwill. Do I have your understanding?"

Sigurd nodded.

"It took you a long time to build this, didn't it?" Lucifer asked, his eyes scanning the polished wood.

"Coming by the appropriate resources is difficult," Sigurd mumbled.

"Well, I cannot say I left here and you remained completely unpunished."

Lucifer snapped his fingers, and the Hell's Horns exploded in a cascade of wood and flesh.

Sigurd was thrown twenty feet by the blast and knocked out.

When he came too, rage consumed him, like he hadn't felt in centuries.

Lucifer was gone and so was the Hell's Horns. The thing that had allowed him to maintain his sanity in the ever-shifting landscape of Hell was obliterated.

Caahra approached and warned Sigurd, "Do not seek vengeance for this. Lucifer is not the man you just saw. The truth of him is much worse. He is unstable and vindictive."

Sigurd picked up a shard of his building.

The wood was so splintered it would be unusable. He'd have to start from scratch.

Sigurd roared in frustration.

He drew his axes and thrust the Hell Key forward.

"Perhaps I have lingered too long. I will not let this go unanswered."

"Where are you going?" Caahra asked, looking alarmed.

"The Ninth Circle of Hell," Sigurd spat.

He dived through the portal.

• • • • •

What happened after that became the stuff of further legend. Some rumours stated that Sigurd matched Lucifer in one-on-one combat, though very few believed this to be true. Some said Lucifer was so impressed with the Viking's courage that he let him live to fight on.

Only Sigurd knew the truth of his encounter with Lucifer. His brazen attack on the three-headed giant in the pit had earned a modicum of the archangel's respect. He only escaped because Lucifer allowed him to, a fact Sigurd was well aware of.

In the centuries that followed, Sigurd began work on reconstructing the Hell's Horns. It took a long time, but Sigurd had time to spare and nothing else to do.

Once it was done, Sigurd was rarely seen there.

He devoted himself to finding a way out of Hell, though none of the ancient doors he discovered would open to a dead man. He travelled old forgotten roads in the wasteland and dived deep into unknown caves. There were lands and ruins completely ignored by Lucifer because they weren't within the boundaries of the nine rings.

Still, his search proved frustratingly fruitless, but he didn't stop.

And so he lingered, a warrior without a purpose and a king without a country, right up until the modern day.

CHAPTER 16

THE YEAR 2021

The day started like every other day had for such a long time.

Sigurd rose from his bed, feeling temporarily alive, before remembering he was dead.

He looked out of his roughly hewn windows at the perpetually red stormy sky.

A horde of the primal, animalistic demons could be heard chattering somewhere nearby. They'd learned long ago to avoid Sigurd's house, lest they end up missing a limb or two.

Sigurd had fallen into a slump. He sparingly went to the Hell's Horns these days as the demonic tavern was more a product of Sodom than his.

He often dreamt of riding into battle with Gunnar and Hogni at his side. Memories of another life so distant they didn't seem real.

He missed Gudrun immensely and often regretted that he

hadn't taken the chance to speak with Brynhild on the Road to Hel. Her anger in life had been partly his fault and he'd had the chance to fix it in death, yet had been too much of a coward. These long years without love weighed heavily on him. Even the detachedness of death couldn't completely dim this feeling. He wondered what had happened on her journey, since he'd never seen her again.

Sigurd chuckled when he mused that normally men became lost in life, but he was lost in death. Even the wisdom he'd gained from the heart of Fafnir couldn't generate a solution in his brain.

His silver axes, now an ancient gift from the Goddess of Death, had lost their gleam recently. They were now incredibly old, and their magic was starting to fade.

Sigurd hoped that if the borders to Hell ever reopened, an imp or a demon might find Gram and bring it to him. Though, he figured the sword was now rusted and destroyed beyond recognition.

Sigurd had gone from a general to a dragon-slayer, a king, a barman, a rat in the walls, then to a Hell-warrior. He didn't know where he was to go from here.

Sometimes he liked to sit with Caarha, the succubus, and discuss these things. Ever since the day he'd saved her, she'd always been willing to talk things over. Though the wisdom of demons was, regrettably, somewhat lacking in some subjects. They were created with a purpose and never had to find it.

Sigurd put on his sling and grabbed his axes. He never wore armour anymore. Nothing in Hell was foolish enough to attack him. And, as of Lucifer's orders, he stayed well away from the Knights of Hell.

Resolving to visit the Hell's Horns and fight away his blues,

Sigurd thrust the white Hell Key forward and stepped into the breach it summoned.

When he arrived in Sodom, he was horrified at what he saw.

Sigurd looked in dismay at the missing outer wall of the Hell's Horns.

Part of the tavern had been blown apart. Kanto and Caarha were nowhere to be seen.

There was only one being who dared to insult Sigurd like this.

After all these years, Lucifer still thought it okay to play games with him.

He'd committed the infernal construction the second time over to better accommodate the demons, no matter how ghastly he personally found them, and still his tavern was a target for attack.

Sigurd grasped the Hell Key dangling around his neck. He thrust it forward again, generating a portal to the Ninth Circle of Hell. Through the spinning tear in reality, he saw the dark frozen wasteland Lucifer called home.

Sigurd wondered if this was the way it was always going to be. A never-ending battle between himself and Lucifer until the end of time.

Was this how the story of Sigurd the Volsung ended?

He did not care anymore.

Sigurd had some words to share with the Prince of Darkness, and he wasn't going to do it politely.

The giant red monster was torturing some poor soul caught in his grip. It was a young black haired girl, who almost seemed alive...

For all Sigurd cared, Lucifer could finish his business with the poor soul later.

He readied his axes.

"This time, you will learn, Lucifer," Sigurd stated as he dived through the portal into the cold abyss below.

SIGURD'S STORY CONTINUES IN:

THE OLD WORLD SAGA BOOK FOUR:

FALL SILVER
ARTEMIS

THE OLD WORLD SAGA SO FAR...

BOOK ONE: IN THE SHADOW OF MONSTROUS THINGS

A European holiday takes a sinister turn when Joshua Dare encounters a werewolf. Feeling its bite, Josh escapes, but soon realises that he is now inflicted with an ancient curse. Having to learn how to manage his full moon affliction, Josh is thrust into a world of secret organisations, government operatives and mysterious strangers hunting him. Josh has entered a larger story of gods and monsters, and this is just the beginning...

NOVELLA ONE: THE WENDIGO INCIDENT

Something has angered a supernatural terror in the forests of Minnesota, and the US Government needs help dealing with it. Fortunately, rumours have reached them that the Australians have captured a werewolf. Sometimes to kill a monster, you need a monster of your own. Now, Joshua Dare is off to the USA to assist in bringing down one of Native American folklore's greatest monsters - the wendigo. Other sinister things seem to be happening in that forest too....

Book Two: RISE GOLDEN APOLLO

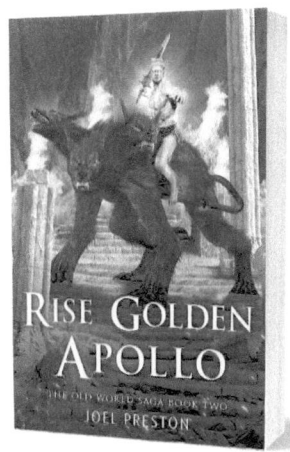

RISE GOLDEN APOLLO follows the two stories simultaneously. Join Melissa Pythia as she searches for a powerful artefact in Rome. More than underworld figures are on her trail as she learns about her connection to a golden sword.

At the same time follow the gods of the Underworld as they wage war against the angels of Heaven. The surprise attack on the Olympians leaves Apollo lost in time. Only Melissa can bring him back...

Book Three: IN THE SHADOW OF THE OLD WORLD

Fearing an information leak and seeking to bolster their alliance with The Old World, the Australian Government has moved Josh Dare to Japan. He is soon tracked down by malevolent supernatural forces who want to exploit his curse. He is the best link to the empty position of Zeus, the vanished god-king. Now, a small team of Australian and US operatives need to work with the gods of old to fulfil an ancient ritual and stop that power falling into the wrong hands.